MW01245698

The Transnational – A Literary Magazine

Vol. 1

Imprint/Impressum

editor:

Sarah Katharina Kayß

Dennis Staats

translation:

Seong-Ho Kwak (UK)

Ariane Enkelmann (Germany)

graphic design:

Dennis Staats (Austria)

photography:

Sarah Katharina Kayß (UK)

PR-work

Dennis Staats (Austria)

Herstellung und Verlag: BoD – Books on Demand, Norderstedt

ISBN: 9783732299416

Bibliografische Information der Deutschen Nationalbibliothek: Die Deutsche Nationalbibliothek verzeichnet diese Publikation in der Deutschen Nationalbibliografie; detaillierte bibliografische Daten sind im Internet über www.dnb.de abrufbar.

Lieber Leser, liebe Autoren,

Im Frühjahr hat PostPoetry Menschen aus der ganzen Welt dazu aufgerufen kreativ zu werden und uns mitzuteilen, was sie sagen würden, wenn sie in 20 Sekunden eine Nachricht an die gesamte Weltbevölkerung richten könnten. In Zeiten der Globalisierung, der kontinuierlichen Auflösung nationaler Grenzen, der Zunahme transnationaler Studiengänge, dem Ausbau von transnationalen Informationssystemen und Organisationen, dachte ich, es wäre eine großartige Möglichkeit, die Chance zu bekommen, (sich vorzustellen) zu allen Menschen auf dieser Welt sprechen zu können. Sich mitzuteilen. Etwas Wichtiges los zu werden. Vielleicht auch etwas Lustiges. Etwas Ernstes. Oder sich einfach nur selbst vorzustellen. Irgendwas (Kreatives). Wir haben fast hundert Antworten erhalten. Darunter nicht eine einzige die ich mit in die erste Ausgabe des Transnational hätte mit aufnehmen wollen.

Der überwiegende Teil der Autoren versuchte die Möglichkeit zu nutzen heimatlose Gedichte an den Mann zu bringen, die mit dem Thema aber unschlüssiger Weise nicht einmal etwas zu tun hatten.

Ein großer Teil gab an 20 Sekunden lang zu schweigen. Gar nichts zu sagen. Damit hatte ich nicht gerechnet, schließlich wächst unsere Welt doch zunehmend zusammen: wir werden global(er), jetten um den gesamten Erdball und vernetzen uns über die nationalen Grenzen hinaus nicht nur sozial, sondern auch wirtschaftlich und nicht zuletzt kulturell. Nimmt man die eingereichten Antworten nun alle zusammen, scheint es allerdings so, als hätten wir einander nicht viel zu sagen. Oder zumindest nichts Wichtiges. Macht ein Zusammenwachsen der Erdbevölkerung dann überhaupt Sinn?

Seitdem ich in London, in der wohl multikulturellsten Metropole Europas lebe, fällt mir immer wieder auf, wie die Menschen einzelner Nationalitäten einander suchen, sich finden und dann (soziale) Gruppen und Netzwerke erschaffen, die alles andere als multikulturell sind. Seltsam ist es - gerade hier, wo sie alle beisammen sind, vom Kanadier zum Chilenen, vom Norweger zum Südafrikaner und vom Australier zum Russen. Hier, wo die Menschen zeigen könnten, dass eine multikulturelle Gesellschaft wirklich funktionieren kann. Aber die meisten tun es nicht. Nicht nur ganze Stadtteile formen sich im Rahmen homogener Nationalitäten,- auch das Berufs- und Universitätsleben ist geprägt durch Interessensgruppen, die sich ganz gerne an Rasse, Religion oder Nationalität orientieren. Warum ist das so? Wollen wir einander nicht kennen lernen?

Hilary Swank sagte einmal „Ich bete für den Tag, an dem wir nicht nur unsere Unterschiede akzeptieren, sondern unsere Verschiedenheit zelebrieren können." Wie sollen wir das tun, wenn es an unserer Kommunikation schon scheitert? Und, um auf den ersten Punkt zurückzukommen, vielleicht haben wir uns ja nichts zu sagen. Aber warum schweigen wir? Weil es uns zu anstrengend ist? Weil uns Unbekanntes unheimlich ist? Warum? Keine der Antworten konnte diese Frage für mich beantworten. Nicht eine einzige.

Spannender Weise haben einige der Europäer ihre Antwort mehrsprachig eingesandt, während die US-Amerikanischen Einsendungen alle auf Englisch ankamen. Was bedeutet das? Dass sich die Europäer Gedanken gemacht haben, dass man sie in ihrer Muttersprache nicht weltweit verstehen kann? Und wenn ja, warum denken die Amerikaner dann, dass man Englisch überall versteht? Verstehen wir einander – und wollen wir dies überhaupt? Das ist eine Frage, die wir uns vielleicht zwangsläufig stellen müssen: Sind uns die ganzen transnationalen Strömungen im 21. Jahrhundert unheimlich oder müssen wir uns an Grenzöffnungen zunächst gewöhnen? Und wenn ja, wollen wir uns überhaupt daran gewöhnen?

Der Transnational ist ein Heft, das vor allem kulturell unterschiedlich geprägte Lyrik mit einem politischen oder sozialkritischen Fokus über die nationalen Grenzen hinaus ins Zentrum stellen wird. Der Fokus ist daher global – kulturübergreifend. Aber geht das überhaupt? Sind wir im Inbegriff dessen, unsere Grenzen zu öffnen, uns einander näher zu kommen und dann schlussendlich doch da zu stehen und nichts zu sagen zu haben: Eben NICHTS – „nichts" war die häufigste Antwort auf unsere Frage … Haben wir uns wirklich nichts zu sagen?

Die Globalisierung ist nicht im Anmarsch: Sie steht bereits vor der Tür … und was machen wir in dem Moment, wenn wir länger als 20 Sekunden miteinander sprechen müssen?

Viel Spaß mit der Erstausgabe des Transnational,

Dear readers and contributors,

Earlier this year, PostPoetry asked people all over the world to get creative and let us know what they would say if they had 20 seconds to address the entire world population. In these times of globalisation, continual dissolution of national boundaries, proliferation of transnational degree programmes and the expansion of international information systems and organisations, I thought it would be a great opportunity to imagine speaking to every person on the planet. To express yourself. To get something important off your chest. To say something funny, perhaps, or something serious. Or to say something creative. Or maybe just to introduce yourself. Anything (creative) really. We received nearly a hundred responses. Out of all of these, there wasn't a single one I actually wanted to print.

Most people tried to use the opportunity to submit their unpublished poems that, for some bizarre reason, didn't even have anything to do with the question.

A lot of people said they would remain silent for 20 seconds. Without saying a single word. That was something I hadn't expected, since our world is growing increasingly closer: we're becoming (more) global, flying all over the world, creating links across national borders, in social, economic and cultural terms. But when I looked at all the answers submitted, it seemed as though we didn't have much to say to each other after all. Or at least nothing of importance. If that's the case, does it make sense for the world population to continue to grow closer together?

Ever since I started living in London, one of the most multicultural cities in Europe, I've noticed how people of different nationalities look for each other, find each other and then create (social) groups and networks which are anything but multicultural. It's strange – especially here, where we're all gathered together, from Canadians to Chileans, Norwegians to South Africans and Australians to Russians. This is a place where people have the opportunity to show that a multicultural society really can work. But most people don't. It's not just whole neighbourhoods that are formed on the basis of homogenous nationalities – universities and workplaces are defined by interest groups who align themselves in terms of ethnic origin, religion or nationality. Why? Do we just not want to get to know each other?

Hilary Swank once said, "I pray for the day when we not only accept our differences but we actually celebrate our diversity." How can we do that if we fail to communicate with each other? Going back to my earlier point, maybe we don't actually have anything to say to each other. But why do we remain silent? Because it's difficult? Because we're wary of what we don't know? Why? None of the responses we received could answer that question for me. Not a single one.

Interestingly, some of the Europeans sent their responses in different languages, whereas the American submissions were all in English. What does that mean? That Europeans have thought about the fact that people all over the world might not understand their mother tongue? And if so,

why do Americans think that people all over the world understand English? Do we understand each other at all – and do we want to? This is a question which we must perhaps ask ourselves: are we scared by the transnational trends of the 21st century or do we need more time to get used to barriers being opened? And if so, do we even want to get used to this?

The Transnational is a magazine which puts culturally diverse poetry into the limelight, focussing on political or socio-critical poetry that transcends national borders. So our remit is global – extending across cultures. But is that even possible? Are we about to open our borders and grow closer only to stand opposite each other in the end and have nothing to say: absolutely NOTHING – *nothing* was the most common response to our question. Do we really have nothing to say to each other?

Globalisation is not something that's about to happen: it's something that's happening right now … so what are we going to do when we're forced to talk to each other for longer than 20 seconds?

Have fun with the first edition of the Transnational,

Sarah Katharina Kayß
(editor | Herausgeberin)

Table of Contents/Inhalt

ANGELA S. PATANE |

harbor house

I got my period at 11. My mother said, "I hope you don't leave bloody underwear on your bedroom floor for the dog to chew." I would have to wear crotchless rags to school. I grew up never wearing panties. I'd bunch my knickers in corners, but the dog would always find them, lured in by unwashed towels, cheerleading socks, cups, pens, dust, paper, purses, make-up, sneakers, flip-flops, bathing suits, bras, pictures, magazines, weed, bong water, beer, chips, cookie crumbs, clay, fake silver, head bands, pajamas, cigarettes, and old coffee. Now, I own the house. The front door's key reads Defiant, the master bedroom's Fruitless. Odd embossing for unlocking in the dark. Renters get wordless copies. I pay the mortgage, but I never learned to clean the tub. What began as an act of defiance— the clutter, the dust, the bloody rags— kept me a child who can't care for herself. Morganne, my roommate, 22, two years my junior, taught me to clean my tub with Ajax and a sponge and rubber gloves because I've never trusted anyone over 30. Tenant friends, lovers, drug users, aliens, magicians, artists, shape shifters, and pedagogues move in and out around me. They leave TVs—I have six!—broken microwaves, power tools, shoes, mirrors, school projects, knobs, lamps, chairs, empty bottles, dressers, coffee pots, ceramics, street signs, paint, CDs, desks, movies, clocks, and cook books. My house is a harbor for their abandoned possessions. Unable to decide what's worth keeping, I cling to it all. If I dump the junk lining the garage walls, I'll stop getting yeast infections. I'll put my face to the cold, clean cement floor and for the first time feel this space for which I am responsible.

the last hetero on earth

My brother didn't become gay. He was that way before the fight between Mama and Papa, as they were about to separate, when Mama said to my brother through sobbing mouth mucus, "I hope you aren't like him! If you are, you better figure it out before you get married and ruin some woman's life." I was there, but blocked it out. Papa reminded me after my brother came out to us, as he was preparing to tell my mother. "He's afraid," Papa said. "You don't remember her hoping he wasn't like me?" My brother was seventeen. I was twelve. My brother said, "I'm not, Mommy; I'm not." It came back to me. I wonder what my brother remembers. He found Papa's magazines in the office desk at thirteen as he helped at the real estate business after school. We all stuffed envelopes, but my brother kept up the computers. Mama made a big deal about my brother having found the evidence and holding it in since eleven. Little did she know my isolation while doors were locked and yelling seeped through the frames. To them I was too young to know. I was left alone. At twenty-five my brother finally figured it out, after years of leaving coeds in hotel rooms to smoke cigarettes because he couldn't get it up. That's when we became friends. When my brother finally told Mama, she was the last to know. She called me the last hetero on earth. She said, "Every man I have ever known has abandoned me." That's where I got that from. Now Christ is the only man in her life. I told her what her marriage showed me: "You have yourself, your mind, your body. No man will make you complete."

zufluchtsort

Ich habe meine Tage mit 11 bekommen. Meine Mutter sagte, „Lass deine blutige Unterwäsche nicht in deinem Zimmer liegen, sonst zerkaut der Hund sie." Ich musste dann extradicke Vorlagen zur Schule tragen. Als Kind hatte ich nie Unterhosen getragen. Ich knüllte meine Schlüpfer in die Ecke, aber der Hund fand sie immer, weil er angelockt wurde von schmutzigen Handtüchern, Sportsocken, Bechern, Stiften, Staub, Papier, Handtaschen, Make-Up, Turnschuhen, Flip-Flops, Badeanzügen, BHs, Bildern, Zeitschriften, Gras, Bongwasser, Bier, Chips, Kekskrümeln, Lehm, unechtem Silber, Haarreifen, Schlafanzügen, Zigaretten und altem Kaffee. Das Haus gehört jetzt mir. Auf dem Haustürschlüssel steht *Dickköpfig*, auf dem zum Schlafzimmer *Unproduktiv*. Seltsamer Aufdruck, um im Dunkeln aufzuschließen. Mieter bekommen sie wortlos nachgemacht. Ich bezahle die Hypothek, aber ich habe nie gelernt, wie man die Badewanne putzt. Durch den Ungehorsam von früher – die Unordnung, den Staub, die blutigen Vorlagen – bin ich ein Kind geblieben, das nicht für sich selbst sorgen kann. Morganne, meine Mitbewohnerin, 22, zwei Jahre jünger als ich, hat mir gezeigt, wie man die Wanne mit Ajax und einem Schwamm und Gummihandschuhen schrubbt, denn ich habe mich nie jemandem über 30 anvertraut. Befreundete Mieter, Geliebte,

Drogenabhängige, Ausländer, Zauberer, Künstler, Gestaltwandler und Pädagogen ziehen um mich herum ein und aus. Sie hinterlassen mir Fernseher – ich habe sechs! – kaputte Mikrowellen, Elektrowerkzeug, Schuhe, Spiegel, Schulprojekte, Ständer, Lampen, Stühle, leere Flaschen, Kommoden, Kaffeetassen, Porzellan, Straßenschilder, Farbe, CDs, Schreibtische, Filme, Uhren und Kochbücher. Mein Haus ist ein Zufluchtsort für ihr zurückgelassenes Hab und Gut. Weil ich mich nicht entscheiden kann, was davon es wert ist, es zu behalten, halte ich an allem fest. Wenn ich den Müll, der die Garagenwände säumt, wegwerfe, bekomme ich keine Pilzinfektionen mehr. Dann lege ich mein Gesicht auf den kalten, sauberen Zementfußboden und spüre zum ersten Mal diesen Ort, für den ich verantwortlich bin.

der letzte Hetero auf Erden

Mein Bruder wurde nicht schwul. Er war schon so, bevor Mama und Papa sich stritten, als sie kurz davor waren, sich zu trennen, und als Mama zu meinem Bruder verheult und den Mund vom Heulen voller Schleim sagte, „ Ich hoffe du bist nicht so wie er! Wenn du so bist, dann solltest du das rausfinden, bevor du heiratest und das Leben einer Frau zerstörst." Ich war dabei, habe es aber verdrängt. Papa erinnerte mich daran, nachdem mein Bruder sich vor uns geoutet hatte, und plante, es meiner Mutter zu erzählen. „Er hat Angst," sagte Papa. "Erinnerst du dich nicht daran, dass sie wollte, dass er nicht so ist wie ich?" Mein Bruder war siebzehn. Ich war zwölf. Mein Bruder sagte, "Ich bin nicht so,

11

Mami; wirklich nicht." Es fiel mir wieder ein. Ich frage mich, ob mein Bruder sich daran erinnert. Als er dreizehn war, fand er Papas Zeitschriften in der Schreibtischschublade, als er nach der Schule im Maklerbüro aushalf. Der Rest von uns hat Briefe verpackt, aber mein Bruder hat sich um die Computer gekümmert. Mama machte einen Aufstand, weil mein Bruder die Beweise gefunden und seit er elf war versteckt hatte. Sie ahnte nichts von meiner Einsamkeit vor verschlossenen Türen, durch deren Rahmen das Geschrei sickerte. Ihrer Meinung nach war ich zu jung, um das mitzubekommen. Ich wurde in Ruhe gelassen. Als er fünfundzwanzig war, fand mein Bruder es letztendlich heraus, nachdem er jahrelang Kommilitoninnen rauchend in Hotelzimmern zurückgelassen hatte, weil er keinen hochkriegte. Damals wurden wir Freunde. Als mein Bruder es Mama endlich erzählte, war sie die Letzte, die es erfuhr. Sie nannte mich den letzten Hetero auf Erden. Sie sagte, "Alle Männer, die ich je kannte, haben mich verlassen." Da habe ich das her. Jetzt ist Christus der einzige Mann in ihrem Leben. Ich habe ihr erzählt, was ihre Ehe mich gelehrt hat: "Du hast dich selbst, deinen Geist und deinen Körper. Kein Mann wird dich je vervollständigen."

ANTHONY KEATING |

remembrance day

I knew them in my youth, old soldiers,
Senses so basted with horror
that sleep tortured them,
Regulars of libraries, benches and public bars,
Lonely men, that ate in hot plate cafes.

Forgotten and shunned,
Grateful to talk with an ardent boy,
Unaware their currency was so debased,
They spoke of gas and Wizz-Bangs,
Comrades and waste,
Testifying against the myth of eternal youth,
Having eaten bully beef amongst its fetid decay.

And now the last of them is in the barracks of the dead,
We fawn on their memory having ignored the lives
The odd, the lonely, disfigured and mad,
Regiments that marched from bedsits to paupers graves,
Without wreath, flags or tears,

But let us sound the bugle and let rip the drum,
Sing laments and marching songs,
Those who lived the truth have departed.
So let us remember them,
At the going down of the sun
and in the morning,
But above all honour their memory,
By recognising the stench of
the old lie:
Dulce et decorum est Pro patria mori,
Be it in Latin, German, English, French,
Or a thousand other tongues.

the difference between

The bomb maker
Takes pride in the work,
Considers the target,
Timer, detonator,
Container, Explosive,
Shrapnel and direction of blast,
-All to maximize the kill-

A failsafe will be crafted
To protect the foot soldier
Who will place the bomb
And set the charge
-A soldier blown up
In a cheap hotel
Is no martyr at all-

The possibility of defusing
Must be factored in.
    If attempted the device
        Must be wired
         To fool the enemy,
         And snuff out their life
        -For small victories
        Are better than none-

        Fail or succeed
        'Professionally'
        The desire is for the work
        To be admired,
        -As a masterpiece in fragments
        Or a masterpiece disarmed-

        The foot soldier
        Must think of nothing but the
        cause,
        Or the bomb, for all its craft,
        Will be tossed into a canal,
        To rust, decay or explode,
        Killing a few fish
        -Who are not, after all,
        Human like him-

BART BULTMAN |

what is progress?

What is progress?
When recent meteorite did strike our face,
How many witches did we burn?
How many gods sighted us with
unleashed anger?
How many sinners of shakable faith were
tested?
None,
As progress has been made.
But now, fair people, the question to
answer:
Which is the faster,
Us?
Or that which surrounds us?

Was ist Fortschritt?

Was ist Fortschritt?
Wenn der Meteorit erst kürzlich unser
Gesicht gestreift hat,
Wie viele Hexen haben wir verbrannt?
Wie viele Götter haben unseren
entfesselten Zorn zu Gesicht bekommen?
Wie viele Sünder erschütterbaren
Glaubens wurden geprüft?
Kein Einziger,
Während der Fortschritt erfolgt ist.
Und jetzt, ihr Lieben, die Frage bleibt:
Was ist schneller,
Wir?
Oder das, was uns umgibt?

CHRIS SITEMAN |

3 poems for the money god

Capitalists possess an oceanic patience for poems. After all,
capital wants to know the point, how to profit from answers,
and poems give most useful answers.

> I often pay my taxes & rent with poems. My wife's dentist bill?
> Paid-in-full with sonnets. I've typed my gas tank full with haikus,
> paid parking tickets with epigrams.

Poems draft perfect for engineering bulldozers. Often turned
into chainsaws & used to clear cut forests, they're absolute
as blacktop. High schools, auto-

> Ecstatic nasal voices extend lines of credit over the phone
> based on the long term equity built up in my poems. I slip
> lyrics into the collection tray at mass:

factories & office parks: you name what's made from poems.
Houses built of poems withstand hurricanes. Emergency
shelter poems come triage unit equipped.

> altar boys turn cartwheels. In front of the emergency room doors,
> holding my broken jaw, I read a sign: *Poets welcome.*
> *Health rendered on a poem by poem basis.*

Poems can be coiled into razor-wire, fired from machine guns,
or used to inter enemy combatants. Topnotch for bagging
bodies. Plus, they sop up blood very well.

> Even my mechanic refuses anything more than ballads as payment.
> When I look at my bank statement, I cringe with guilty thoughts
> at the rate of return on the dividends I'll earn

A smart investment for those looking to diversify
their holdings in these troubling & uncertain times.

> from my investments in Form & Function, Inc.,
> for I only hear verses that end slant rhyme.

the bindery

1.

In the photo I'm seven. It's Saturday, &
my father sits beside me on the steps at
Lake Fire Road.
I smell his salt skin, Old Spice, a Winston
burning low. On his arm, Ajax tattooed
in gothic script. Two pupils pierce the
smoke—

Darkness even shadows couldn't escape.
You hear people talk about climbing walls—
I climbed walls.

To taste ink & sweat brings back the
noon whistle, the porch railing I think I
clutched for years
as a seven-year-old. His cracked lips smile,
speak the wish he could take back
his blood & sweat: *I lived to die in debt.*

2.

The boy held the gun, crying at the all too
real mess heads made.
Cars arrived, blues flashing, tires
crunching the gravel drive—

***

Who fathered the man who fathered me?
Whispering close to my face about
smashmouth
basketball games on concrete courts, his
razor-wire irises froze my soul.

***

Part of me believes my father incapable of
killing. Another part believes he turned
the gun
against himself, wrote his blood name on
that wall, a Gorgon's head, a mirror &
trophy
for the man whose stains even mighty
AJAX couldn't bleach out.

3.

The Bit O' Honey my father & I shared
on that car ride to the city remains
the sun's warmth on my legs, each sliver a
Saturday morning to carry with me.

Steel drums, inks & acids, concrete,
fluorescent lights, presses, cutters, folders,
hydraulic skids, pallets of paper—

We played guns with rubber bands long as
my seven-year-old arms. Our laughter
rang
like shrieks from the gulls we threw pizza
crusts to
out the window, & they'd catch &
swoop—

Feathers snapping, fluttering, tucked into
air, beaks arrowing, falling stares—
Pure vertigo in shafts of light, hung there,
then darted from sight.

4.

At lunch the pressmen & cutters let me be, but
one day want me to come to where the windows
overlook the dormitories at MIT.

Part of me believes they knew we could see.
Another part believes they didn't care,
or liked to be watched.

All us workers lined the windows eating &
staring from an entire world away.

Those beautiful young girls, even if they knew they
were beautiful, never knew
how beautiful they were to us on break from
machines demanding we be machines.

5.

My father liked playing the girl in the
children's poem that kept picking her

15

nose
until the razor-toothed monster in her
nostril bit the top digit off.

Weeks after the bandages, the nub still
looked like bone
pushing through, & he'd pretend to pick,
then pull
his chopped pinky out with an *Ouch*!

Our bodies jiggled with laughter, but
when I asked what happened, his brow
tensed, he spoke very close to my face: *I
told you, a monster lives up there*—

6.
My father killed himself so slowly no one
noticed. So, he kept living,
at holidays still scarfs second servings of
turkey. I bear witness—

He sweat & bled to pay our rent, never
bitched about eating dogs & beans,
read Tom Clancy on the can & died a
prisoner to a factory clock.

His gravel voice whispered bones,
whispered blood. His hands wore ink
stains. He lived
a child of metaphor, offspring of inmates
& guards.

In the end my father earned the grave he
sought, & knows no need of these
benedictions.

7.
Down to the side like the razor-edge on a
book-cutter's blade, I remember growing
up
with my father on Lake Fire Road, & my
face shows me his face.

Seventy hours a week he labored as a

bookbinder, & lost parts unsaveable
by surgeons with a hundred texts on
suture.

When we wrestled he'd rear on his knees
like a bear & roar, tickling
until we thrashed, too speechless to beg
him to stop.

Now, my best hopes set the machinery of
mills & presses in motion—
Betrayal & gift sending men like him to
their bindery.

"The Bindery" was first published in Anomalous #5

the gate is wide

Vulcan rains fire on ants; a boy Zippos
hairspray,
watches bodies burn outside a housing
block;
a thousand buttons snap against the cold.
***
Charred soldiers guard a desert crossroads
where shelled roads part. A red finger-
paint sign:

Everything must go—

COLLEEN M. FARRELLY |

homecoming king

our homecoming king
hailed honored as a leader
you chose leadership
and at your next home coming
we protested that honor

Heimgekehrter König

unser heimgekehrter König
gefeiert verehrt als anführer
wähltest du führerschaft
und bei deinem nächsten heimspiel
bestritten wir diese ehre

***

This poem is about a friend of mine, now a retired infantryman. He was quite popular and involved in his high school before enlisting (sports, school dances...); however, when he came home from his first tour in Iraq, he did not receive the same sort of welcome as he did in high school. The poem was written after a discussion with a few friends about coming home to communities that didn't understand, divorce papers, student loan/apartment issues that had occurred while deployed... C.M.F.

In diesem Gedicht geht es um einen meiner Freunde, mittlerweile ein ehemaliger Soldat. Bevor er sich zum Wehrdienst verpflichtet hatte, war er beliebt gewesen und hatte sich viel in seiner Schule engagiert (Sportmannschaften, Schulveranstaltungen…); als er allerdings von seinem ersten Einsatz im Irak zurückkehrte, wurde er nicht auf dieselbe Art und Weise willkommen geheißen wie damals in der Schule. Das Gedicht entstand nach einem Gespräch mit einigen Freunden über die Heimkehr zu Menschen, die einfach nicht verstanden, Scheidungspapiere, Studiendarlehens-/Wohnungsprobleme während seiner Stationierung im Ausland…

ever after

Her glass slipper turns to his M16,
her elegant dress to faded fatigues.
He's a shell of the man from their intrigues,
served five months patrol away from his queen.

Cinders to palace, her dreams now rubble,
she watches her carriage morph to Abrams tank,
as if her fairy tale were some cruel prank.
He shouts, "Hurry, men! March on the double!"

Her clock strikes twelve, his tank an IED,
and widower's daughter is left widow.
She has but memories, now as shadows,
to comfort her dark days of misery.
Her ever after has no tomorrow,
leaving Juliet her grief and sorrow.

prince and princess

I stare blankly at the teens in the picture.
Her cheeks are rosy as she laughs and
dances
the night away with Prince Charming, sure
her dresses, her flowers, and their romance
will stand the test of time. He smiles; the
contours
of his tux-vest catch light as time advances
relentlessly, cutting short their special
night.
They are blissfully blind to their future
plight.

One short year past, fate has separated by
time and place, introducing a now and
then—
before and after—the dogs of war decreed
youth's bitter end. No more can they
pretend
to be prince and princess. On bended
knee,
both beg for peace and a chance to amend
the wrongs witnessed, just wrongs
committed—
by him, by her—those wrongs never
remitted.

I stare vacantly at that picture, and my
former self smiles back as she dances the
night
away with her Prince Charming. She buys
into youth's lie; yet, I admire her light
and optimism, her dreamer's lullaby
lolloping across the dance floor. We must
fight
our biggest fight to regain those dreams,
that life,
if we are to overcome war's hidden strife.

Prinz und Prinzessin

Ich starre die Teenies auf dem Bild leer
an. Ihre Wangen sind rot, denn sie lacht
und tanzt
die ganze Nacht durch mit Prinz
Charming, kann sagen,
dass ihre Kleider, ihre Blumen und ihre
Romanze
die Zeiten überdauern werden. Er lächelt;
sein Kragen
spiegelt Licht, die Zeit verrinnt ganz
und erbarmungslos wird ihre große Nacht
verzehrt.
Sie blicken ihrem Gelübde nichtsahnend
entgegen.

Schon ein Jahr später hat das Schicksal in
Zeit und Raum geschieden, ein jetzt und
damals eingeführt – vorher und nachher
– des Krieges Hunde sind das bittere
Ende der Jugend. Nicht länger scheinen
sie, Prinz und Prinzessin zu sein. Auf
Knien betteln beide um Frieden und
wollen vertreiben gesehenes Unrecht,
einfach begangene Fehler – ihre, seine –
Fehler, niemals vergeben.

Ich starre das Bild ausdruckslos an, und
auf
mein lächelndes jüngeres Ich; sie tanzt die
Nacht hindurch mit ihrem Prinz
Charming. Sie kauft der Jugend ihre Lüge
ab; dennoch, ich bewundere ihr Licht und
ihre Zuversicht, ihr Schlaflied vor dem
Traum taumelt über die Tanzfläche. In
unserer größten Schlacht

müssen wir diese Träume, dieses Leben
zurückgewinnen, und so den
hinterhältigen Zwist des Krieges
überwinden.

DARIAN LANE |

making out at spotlights

It wasn't that long ago.

Three months to be exact. I was sitting in Starbucks doing my studies when in walked a short-pale-black-haired-dark eyes-just-my-type-girl. She was staring at me with these dark piercing eyes with black eyebrows that hung like caterpillars. There was a smirk on her face. Like she knew me. Did she know me?
"You don't remember me." She spoke my name.
I stared blankly. She looked familiar, but I couldn't formulate a name or the placement of her face.
"Katherine." She smiled.
My mind raced, Katherine, Katherine, Katherine. Oh, Katherine! The girl I dated for about three weeks until I found out she liked to sleep in closets. Not to mention she had never kissed a guy. At 22 that was quite a feat. This was Katherine's best friend. I met her at a dinner Katherine prepared; Fried Chicken, Watermelon, Biscuits, Cornbread - I tried not to act offended.

"Oh yes, I remember now. Katherine." I struggled to recall this girl's name.
"Courtney." She smirked.
I smirked.
"I'm here to study, mind if I sit here with you, all the tables are full."

We sat in silence for the next 20 minutes pretending to study.

"How is our mutual friend?" I said breaking the stalemate.

"She's good. She's dating someone now."
"Good," I grinned.
She grinned.
"We should hang out sometime." There it was. I had put it out there. And now it was lingering out there like a stench.
"Hmmm..." She pondered.
The waiting was worse than the asking.
"I might have to check with Katherine on that one," she purred with a Colgate smile.

Three hours later we had a date. I arrived promptly at 9:45pm (15 minutes late). She looked at me, sadly; in jeans, t-shirt, hat. She had bought a black dress.
"I thought it was dressy," she said pouty.
"This is California, nothing is dressy. But you look great, lets go." I grabbed her by the arm and whisked her out.

We had fun. We danced, we watched, we kissed, we drank. It was a connection.
"You know, even though Katherine gave me the green light, she had a funny look on her face."
"Sucks to be her." I laughed, pressing my hand onto her bare thigh.
We went home early.

In the car we didn't talk much. Too busy making out at stoplights.

It wasn't until we were in the bedroom half-naked she revealed she was a virgin. Yet I wasn't all that surprised. The surprise came when she rolled on her stomach and asked to be bitten. Curious and intrigued, I obliged.
"Come on, you can do better than that!" With a challenge like that, how could I refuse. The harder I bit, the more turned on she became. Within minutes she exerted a war cry and went limp. I

cuddled up behind, she latched my hand to her breast, and we fell asleep.

In the morning I drove her to her dorm for her Walk Of Shame. We kissed goodbye. It was electric. We kissed again. She looked at me.

She texted the next night, declaring how much she missed sleeping in my bed. The gentleman in me responded/texted, "Get some sleep, you have a final in the morning." (Mistake #1)

The next night...

I'm driving home from work hungry, longing, lonely, "Driving home from work wanna grab a pizza..."
"I'm vegetarian" She texted back.
"They have vegetarian pizzas - lol"
"They do :)"
"I'm driving by the University, do you want me to pick you up..."
No response.

In fact, I didn't hear anything from her until the next morning...

"I get bad cell service here at the University :/" She texted.
It was a lie.
"You do like to play games, don't you..."
" I do" She added a smiley face.
"And here I thought we had something special."
"We don't have anything."
It was a shock. I looked at the phone, the sender, the receiver, the day, the date, the text, the time, it was the end; my ego would never allow me to respond.

celebrity

What's it like being the greatest writer of all time?

I'll tell you.

The Sun, The Moon, The Stars all bow when I exit the apartment. Girls with glasses look at me. Stare. Guys get jealous. Cars stop in the middle of the street. People ask for autographs. Always expecting me to write something snippy or witty. Awkward moments. I just scribble my name.

I never have to buy a drink or pay for a dinner. People are perverse that way. Strangers walk up to me like they know me. The pictures. The pictures. Picture perfect moments that are flawed. Flash.

And the women. Oh, the women. Always asking, When your next project is coming out? I usually hem & haw some obscure answer that gets them all the more curious. The more curious, the more dot dot dot ...

In college I used intellect, charm, pizazz; now I just hand them a short story and watch them foam at the mouth. All it takes is a sentence. A word. A phrase. And the foam starts spewing. Sometimes they break into convulsions from my genius. Almost like an epileptic fit. It is at this point in the conversation I bend over, retrieve my product, meticulously place my phone number in their purse, and step over them as I walk through the double doors into the gleaming light of my greatness...

There is however a seamy side. People always try to copy my work. Talentless People. Bitter; they create labels for you, labels like: arrogant, self-serving, misogynistic, asshole. Their overly read intellect will not allow them to appreciate the innovative, the mind-boggling sheer power of my writing. Sometimes they'll even try to compare me to another author; thus giving off the subliminal message I copied that writer. Nobody writes like me, I tell them. Nobody.

As a child I used to stare into the mirror and ask myself…"Vincent, you genius of a writer you, what would you rather have … success 'or' be known as the greatest writer of all time?" In a flash I had the answer. Immediately I dropped to my knees and begged God to grant me talent over success. God has answered that prayer. Yet I question it everyday.

Celebrity

Wie isses denn so, wenn man der beste Schriftsteller aller Zeiten ist?

Ich sag's dir.

Die Sonne, der Mond und alle Sterne beugen sich, wenn ich meine Wohnung verlasse. Mädels schauen mich durch Gläser an. Starren. Männer werden eifersüchtig. Autos halten auf der Mitte der Straße an. Menschen bitten mich um Autogramme. Erwarten, dass ich was Kurzes oder Geistreiches schreibe. Unangenehme Momente. Ich kritzel nur meinen Namen.

Ich muss mir meine Drinks nicht selbst kaufen und bezahle nie für's Abendessen. Menschen sind pervers, wenn es um so

etwas geht. Fremde kommen auf mich zu, als würden sie mich kennen. Die Bilder. Die Bilder. Formen perfekte Bilderbuchmomente, die dennoch unvollkommen sind. Blitz.

Und die Frauen. Mein Gott, die Frauen. Fragen ständig, Wann dein nächstes Projekt abgeschlossen ist? Ich hau meistens ein paar mysteriöse Antworten raus, die sie dann nur noch neugieriger machen. Je neugieriger sie sind, desto mehr Punkt Punkt Punkt …

In der Schule musste ich noch Intelligenz, Charme und Pfiff einsetzen: jetzt gebe ich ihnen nur eine meiner Kurzgeschichten und schau mir an wie sie zu sabbern beginnen. Ein einziger Satz ist völlig ausreichend. Ein Wort. Eine Phrase. Und das Sabbern wird immer mehr. Manchmal bekommen sie Schüttelkrämpfe in Angesicht meiner Genialität. Fast wie ein epileptischer Anfall. Genau an diesem Punkt der Unterhaltung beuge ich mich zu ihnen rüber, hole mir mein Produkt zurück, platziere meine Telefonnummer sorgfältig in ihre Handtasche und steige über sie herüber auf meinem Weg durch die Türen hinein in das schimmernde Licht meiner eigenen Größe…

Trotzdem gibt es auch eine düstere Seite. Menschen versuchen andauernd mich zu kopieren. Talentfreie Menschen. Bitter; denken in Schubladen, so wie: arrogant, eigennützig, frauenfeindlich, Arschloch. Ihr überbelesener Intellekt wird ihnen nicht erlauben, die Innovation und die geistesbetäubende Macht meiner Schreibkunst zu erkennen. Manchmal versuchen sie sogar, mich mit anderen Autoren zu vergleichen; als würden sie mir unauffällig unterstellen ich würde

jemanden kopieren. Aber niemand
schreibt wie ich, sage ich ihnen. Niemand.

Als Kind habe ich immer in den Spiegel
gestarrt und mich gefragt… „Vincent, du
Schreib-Genie, was hättest du lieber…
Erfolg ‚oder‘ als der beste Schriftsteller
aller Zeitenbekannt zu sein?" Wie ein
Blitzschlag kam mir die Antwort. Ich fiel
zu Boden, landete auf meinen Knien und
flehte Gott an, mir mehr Talent zu geben
als Erfolg. Gott hat dieses Gebet erhört.
Und dennoch stelle ich es jeden Tag
meines Lebens in Frage.

DENNIS STAATS |

Bukowski

Ich glaube Bukowski war
ein alter Nazi.

Er verehrte Celine -
irgendwie verständlich -
aber auch der war ein Nazi.

Er las Hamsun
und auch der war einer.

Andererseits mochte
ich meine Großeltern.
Auch die waren Nazis.

Was sagt das
über mich?

Bukowski

I think Bukowski was
an old Nazi.

He admired Celine –
somewhat understandable –
but he, too, was a Nazi.

He read Hamsun
and he was one, too.

On the other hand, I liked
my grandparents.
They, too, were Nazis.

What does that say
about me?

Epitaph

„Entschuldigen Sie bitte,
dass ich nicht aufstehe."

Das hat der alte Hemingway
als seine Grabinschrift festgelegt,
bevor er sich sein versoffenes
Gehirn wegschoss.

Was wird einmal
auf meinem Grabstein stehen?

„Ich trinke aus,
was immer du mir einschenkst."

Yeah, das ist gut. Das gefällt mir.
Denn darum dreht sich doch das Leben.

Mit den Karten zu spielen,
die dir das Leben zuteilt
und zwar so gut es geht.

Ein gutes Spiel.
Ein schneller Drink
Ein kurzer Fick.

Aber wenn sie meinen
von Alkohol aufgedunsenen,
syphilitischen Körper
aus irgendeinem Rattennest ziehen,
dann, mein Freund, wird es Zeit
die Zeche zu zahlen.

Epitaph

"Pardon me
for not getting up."

This is what old Hemingway
intended for his tombstone
before he blew his wasted
brains out.

What will once
be on my tombstone?

"I will finish
every drink you pour me."

Yeah, that's good. I like that.
Because that's what life is all about.

To play the cards
life has dealt you
and as well as you can.

A good game.
A quick drink
A fast fuck.

But when my
syphilitic body,
bloated with alcohol,
is pulled from some rat's nest,
then, my friend, it's time
to pay the price.

JEANINE DEIBEL |

american carnivore

It's not a matter of anthropology. His
pioneers shot
anyone with a bearskin or a stick. They
made good
use of fertility, raised a sufficient army,
and then cut
the king off from his property with the
flex of a red
and blue plume.

The American becomes a marvel, expands
himself
from sea to sea. He grows a ravenous
appetite from all
that traveling and consumes Chinese on
the western front,
loosening his belt a few notches, before
hauling Africa
into the east because outsourcing
provides cheap labor
for tending livestock and slaughtering.

At night, the business of blood saturates
his dreams
and he wakes with a swelling taste for
another cut
craving meat more than a woman, who
surprisingly
is still attracted to him, well to his
affluence anyway,
despite his cascading frame –

belly stretched with sin – the flesh of over
two
hundred pounds per year per person
stuffed into pockets
of skin and soon he stops breeding. He
eats, and eats
alone. He gropes at the globe, his greasy

fingers staining
the third world with chronic poverty, yet
their numbers
grow, penetrate slow

and methodically, until his ever-increasing
need
disbands, competing sectors devour one
other
as mankind revels over the fall of
America, not
the beautiful – but the beast.

deliberate life

Disappointed to say the least
after countless art shows – tracked
interviews – read, loyal subscriber
to the quarterly confident that I could
            count the steps
            as she closed in on genius.

An Archetype of Art
art as art should be, striking up
in me more life than one could
breed in a womb
            I would remind myself,
            stagnant in my own. mess.
of colors.

Publicly poised dashing a hand about to
buyers,
admirers – I saw her at Whitman Gallery
she took leave into the ladies' room
I followed and
            found her snorting off the
vanity
            I held the door for her.

Frustrated for believing that in the 21st
Century

we could reap art from something other than
self-destructive tendencies – my esophagus lost
its length in

        one. long. contraction.

      At home,
           I paint doors

JOE DRESNER |

geological time

The doubt revealed itself like a slip of paper unexpectedly falling out of a book. But still we stumble forward with a sort of joy, like young women sliding through a train station at night on our bare feet in our best dresses with our impractical shoes in our arms. We had been better off participating in those sorts of contests where you guess the number of sweets in a glass jar or the weight of a cake, and if you are correct you get to keep the cake or the jar of sweets, but instead we moved onwards, forwards but also to the side, like a piece in chess or some other board game. And now we lie indolently in the fields which are purely hypothetical, combing the poetry out of hair, with the animals that aren't animals at all.

geologische Zeit

Der Zweifel offenbarte sich wie ein Papierstreifen, der unerwartet aus einem Buch fällt. Und immer noch stolpern wir irgendwie glückselig voran, wie junge Frauen, die nachts barfuß durch einen Bahnhof gleiten, in unseren besten Kleidern mit unseren unpraktischen Schuhen unter den Armen. Es ging uns besser mit Spielen, bei denen man die Süßigkeiten in einem Glas schätzte oder das Gewicht eines Kuchens, und wenn man recht hatte, durfte man den Kuchen oder das Glas Süßigkeiten behalten, doch stattdessen haben wir uns weiterbewegt, vorwärts, aber auch zur Seite, wie eine Spielfigur beim Schach oder einem anderen Brettspiel. Und jetzt liegen wir unbewegt auf rein hypothetischen Feldern, und kämmen die Lyrik aus Haaren, mit den Tieren, die gar keine Tiere sind.

lagom

This is the five-thousand-and-seventy-third time this sort of thing has happened, with their vials of honey and chopped fruit, the crossings back and forth with potted plants, and an imagination shaped by nature yet prone to imperfections.

Besides, when the citizens caught sight of the city they rent their garments in accordance with the best traditions but strangely most wore cool summer clothes, one a pink blouse, another a turquoise sash. You couldn't understand anything said in the ceremony but they gave you a hat for most of it.

Meanwhile the conversation you were having with yourself came to a natural close, as did the day. Thoughts and feelings lingered like music lingering in a theatre even though the spectators are leaving through the vomitorium and the performers have dismantled their instruments.

Tax collectors haunt the mountain passes. The station burns quietly in the background. The women come in twos or threes, driven by curiosity but also a sense of regret, for the cement factory, the dance troupe, the man walking around the perimeter of a field dotted with mounds of snow although the day was mild, perhaps even warm, and soft sounds boomed from the machine in the trees.

Beneath the village was a hill, and beneath that a mine, yet beneath the mine there was a lake with a dark strand and a pier built so that it reached to the centre of the cool water. You could tell there was a story behind it. And there was.

les jeunes nus

The desert doesn't dream of the sea or even of the rain, it instead dreams of other deserts, far colder and vaster than the deserts we ourselves can imagine. Meanwhile our own arrivals at meaning are merely momentary pauses in the on-going dialogue, which steadily accrue like pancakes gradually piling up on the plate, which go well with jam or with syrup, or cheese and bacon. Meanwhile the landscape floods with an almost blinding light. We sometimes feel like an animal whose horns are ineluctably caught up in the bush of what we will one day become. Wait a minute forget that bit. Just remember this.

les jeunes nus

Die Wüste träumt nicht vom Meer oder auch nur vom Regen, sie träumt vielmehr von anderen Wüsten, viel kälter und öder als wir sie uns je selbst vorstellen könnten. Gleichzeitig entstehen jedes Mal, wenn wir einen Sinn erhalten, augenblickliche Pausen im ablaufenden Dialog, die sich stetig summieren, wie ein Pancakestapel, der auf einem Teller emporwächst, der gut zu Marmelade oder Sirup passt, oder zu Käse und Schinken. Gleichzeitig wird die Landschaft mit blendendem Licht überflutet. Manchmal fühlen wir uns wie ein Tier, dessen Hörner sich unvermeidlich im Busch dessen, zu dem wir eines Tages werden, verfangen. Warte vergiss den Teil. Merk dir nur das.

JEFF HARRIS |

The minutia of budget

The minutia of budget making is a big philosophical divide between it and the government, and some of these cabinet members can't get confirmed in this lifetime, but the subcabinet appointments are going forward in a void which is probably a good thing due to the difficult issues facing the slew of other issues on the President's plate. These cabinet members are a slew of bureaucracies that they are running, and even if the decisions aren't being made out of anything anybody can understand, that was not the case under the stewardship of Mighty Moe, but you want to know that the person across from you at the table does, in fact, speak for the President. When it comes to climate change it is clear that the President will get no cooperation from Congress, because people would rather go down with the ship than put their jobs in jeopardy. The Congress would like to get rid of the EPA (Environmental Protection Agency) if they could. This could smooth the way forward for the simmering, basting, and frying of the planet. This is the fast track for getting up there pronto to hang with Jesus. Everything is negotiable with these people, even the laws of physics. Even the best of intentions is not enough. To have someone of that depth of knowledge so close to the oval office is wonderful in a parallelogram-packed universe. Anyway, the race for attention is still alive and well, and protestors are pouring in everywhere. People are being declared dead in the midst of nearly everything. I don't know. I look at you. I see a bubblehead. I don't know. We have fallen short of a majority.

Wie übergenau ein Etat

Wie übergenau ein Etat aufgestellt werden muss, zeigt eine große philosophische Kluft zwischen ihm und der Regierung auf, und einige dieser Kabinettsmitglieder werden in diesem Leben nicht mehr amtlich bestätigt werden, aber die Berufungen ins Unterkabinett füllen ein Vakuum, was wahrscheinlich gut ist, wenn man die schwierigen Themen bedenkt, die der Präsident neben der langen Latte an eigentlichen Themen um die Ohren hat. Diese Kabinettsmitglieder sind die lange Latte an Bürokratien, die sie leiten, und auch wenn Entscheidungen nicht aus irgendwelchen Gründen getroffen werden, die irgendjemand nachvollziehen kann, unter Mighty Moe war das noch anders, möchtest du immerhin trotzdem wissen, dass die Person, die dir da gegenüber sitzt, tatsächlich für den Präsidenten spricht. Wenn es um den Klimawandel geht, ist schon mal klar, dass der Präsident vom Kongress keine Unterstützung zu erwarten hat, denn diese Leute würden lieber mit dem Schiff untergehen, als ihre Jobs zu gefährden. Der Kongress würde auch am liebsten die EPA (Environmental Protection Agency) abschaffen. Das könnte es einfacher machen, den Planeten zu rösten, zu brutzeln und weich zu kochen. Das wäre eine Abkürzung, um ganz fix dort oben bei Jesus rum zu chillen. Mit diesen Leuten kann man für alles einen Kompromiss finden, sogar für die Gesetze der Physik. Sogar die allerbeste Absicht ist nicht ausreichend. Jemanden, der so umfassend gebildet ist, so nah am Oval Office zu wissen, ist wundervoll in einem Universum voller Parallelogramme. Wie auch immer, der Kampf um Aufmerksamkeit ist immer noch im

Gange, und es regnet überall
Demonstranten. Menschen werden
inmitten von fast alldem für tot erklärt.
Ich weiß nicht. Ich sehe dich an. Ich sehe
einen Schwachkopf. Ich weiß nicht. Es
gibt keine Mehrheit mehr.

NICHOLAS KOMODORE |

Elephantiasis

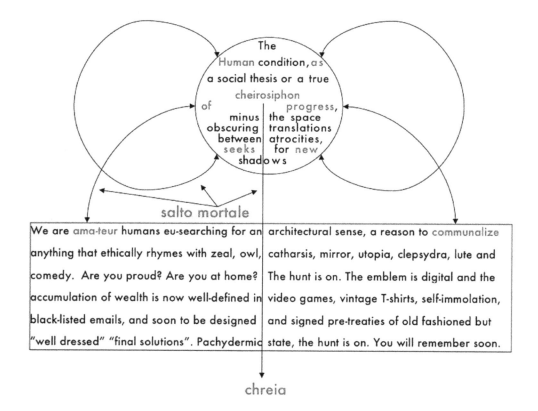

MARK FARRELL |

a kind of ozymandias

"...the greatest qualities a man can have are simplicity and humility..." – Alfred P. Murrah

Rags to riches – Alfred P. Murrah was an all-around success story.
A run-away who made good.
Worked his way through high school,
then college, then was a federal judge
for Oklahoma
(at only thirty-two years of age)
                and stayed on the bench for
over thirty years.
A Democrat. A Methodist. A
Freemason.

Murrah had a building named after him
when he died – a great honour – but it
was also the building that was destroyed
in the Oklahoma City Bombing in 1995.

Today, of course, the bomber, Timothy
McVeigh, is more famous than Alfred
Murrah ever was (and perhaps the U.S.
government made McVeigh even more
famous by executing him).

So,
    does evil triumph over good in the
fame stakes?
Lead an excellent, productive life –
enough to get a federal building named
after you – and then...
                your name is
                        ...eclipsed.

It's nothing to worry about really, I
suppose – it's all out of your hands once
you're dead.

All you can do is
                turn over
in your grave.

Because someone will go and open a
James Joyce Pub in Zurich anyway (or a
James Joyce Café in Trieste) or
                        a Virginia
Woolf's Bar & Bistro in Bloomsbury (with
its renowned To the Lighthouse
Cheeseburger). Oh, this is all true, dear
reader, you can look it up...

And you can also look up Alfred P.
Murrah himself, downgraded now to a
.pdf file on an Oklahoma City Bombing
Memorial website.
The New Federal Building in Oklahoma
City doesn't carry a name.
It's just called:
                The Oklahoma City
Federal Campus.

childish things

I'm in the room of my childhood,
pulling open
the door to the closet there:
        Dozens of board games, role-
playing games.
        A few hundred records.
        At least a thousand comic books.
(All these boxes of things!)
Things that I no longer physically need
as I have everything (and more, much
more)
backed up
burned to
DVDs:

        mp3s, .jpgs and .cbr (comic-book-
reader) files, scans from
BoardGameGeek.com...

All those digital files – little ghosts of all
these boxes of things...
And Mum and Dad – dead within a year
of each other.

Burned.
(Cremated.)
Ghosts.

kindisches zeug

Ich bin im Zimmer meiner Kindheit,
öffne
die Tür zum Wandschrank:
          Dutzende Brettspiele,
Rollenspiele.
          Ein paar hundert Tonaufnahmen.
          Mindestens tausend
Comicbücher.
(All dieses Zeug in Kisten!)
Dinge, die ich wirklich nicht mehr
brauche,
denn ich habe alles (und noch viel, viel
mehr)
gesichert
gebrannt
auf DVDs:

          mp3s, .jpgs und .cbr (comic-
book-reader) Dateien, Scans von
BoardGameGeek.com...

All diese digitalen Dateien – kleine
Schatten von all diesem Zeug in Kisten...
Und Mama und Papa – tot innerhalb
eines Jahres.

Gebrannt.
(Eingeäschert.)
Schatten.

MARTHA CLARKSON |

the lost art of dating

This year I did the unthinkable and forgot
to call my father on his birthday. He was
turning eighty-nine and there were plans
to celebrate a week later when I drove
from Seattle to Portland and those
celebration plans, I imagined, had torn my
focus from remembering the actual day.
My excuses were the same lame lot other
people have; I was drowning in work
email and PowerPoint decks,
compounded by the attention-seeking
vibration of my cell phone. All the things
that have come to be considered 'life in
general.'

Dad and I are cut from the same cloth
when it comes to never forgetting dates
and times, and we certainly never forget
each other's birthdays. He is a card-sender
extraordinaire, not buying any old one,
but going to two or three stores to find
the right one, and if impossible, writing a
limerick inside to combat the banal
printed verbiage. He sends flowers for
special events and last year had a bottle of
champagne waiting in our New York
hotel room to commemorate a work
project my husband was unveiling.

But now I'm sure the real reason I forgot
his birthday is that I never see what day it
is. Rather, what date it is. I used to see it,
everywhere. We all used to. Before
computers set in, I sent five or six faxes a
day from work, each one dated. I had a
calendar hanging on my cubicle wall, a
portable one to take to meetings, and a
glossy photo one adorning my kitchen.
Transmittal cover sheets? Four or five a
day. Letters? A couple. Everything needed

the date. You were desperate to make sure the receiver of your important documents was aware of when you sent it. I carefully hand-wrote those transmittal cover sheets, clipping them to notebooks or reports, and called the bike messenger. I watched the fax machine crank out the beloved receipt that said "message sent," with the date. Receptionists, secretaries, and mail-room boys all over the world slit open envelopes, endured paper cuts, and carefully date-stamped each piece of mail, even the junk. In the unlikely event a day went by that I didn't fax or write letters, I probably wrote a check. And because I saw the date all the time, I was quick to fill in that first empty line: date. For groceries, bills, and dry-cleaning, you wrote checks. Checks were even made out to 'cash' and pushed across the teller line just to get some. With the infrequency I write them now, it takes a second or two of hovering over that first empty line to think of the date.

The date sits down in the lower right corner of computer screens and boldly makes itself known on the home screen of cell phones. But we don't see it. Now, it's the time we pay attention to, as our days shrink down to mattering by the minute.

The night of my father's 89th birthday, I realized my error. Lying in bed at ten, I had to make a choice. Call and wake him and be true to the day, or apologize the heck out of the day after. I chose the latter, because he's eighty-nine and needs his rest, because phone calls in the night can be alarming.

Dad accepted my apology that next morning, but I detected a catch in his still-strong voice. If he'd been with me, the bright red flush in my face would have betrayed my humiliation. Now I have his birthday as a meeting reminder, in caps, on my Outlook calendar, two days before the actual birthday (in time for mailing the card), the day before (for good measure), and the day of. Maybe next year I'll just drive the hundred and eighty miles to see him.

Die verlorene Fertigkeit des Datierens

Dieses Jahr tat ich das Unvorstellbare; ich vergaß, meinen Vater an seinem Geburtstag anzurufen. Er wurde neunundachtzig und wir hatten geplant, eine Woche später, wenn ich von Seattle nach Portland fahren würde, zu feiern, und diese Festpläne, nehme ich an, hatten meine Aufmerksamkeit vom eigentlichen Tag abgelenkt. Meine Entschuldigungen waren der übliche haltlose Haufen; eine Mischung aus einem Sumpf an Arbeitsmails, PowerPoint-Präsentationen und dem nach Aufmerksamkeit heischenden Vibrieren meines Handys. All diese Dinge, die heutzutage als ‚das Leben im Allgemeinen' betrachtet werden.

Vater und ich sind aus dem gleichen Holz geschnitzt, wenn es darum geht, sich ein Datum oder eine Uhrzeit zu merken, und wir würden niemals den Geburtstag des anderen vergessen. Er ist ein Kartenschreiber extraordinaire, er kauft nicht einfach irgendwo, sondern geht in zwei oder drei verschiedene Läden, um die richtige zu finden, und wenn möglich, schreibt er einen Limerick rein, um dem banal gedruckten Geschwafel zu begegnen. Er schickt zu besonderen Anlässen Blumen und letztes Jahr wartete eine Flasche Champagner auf unserem

Hotelzimmer, um ein Arbeitsprojekt zu würdigen, das mein Mann vorgestellt hatte.

Mittlerweile bin ich mir sicher, dass der eigentliche Grund, aus dem ich seinen Geburtstag vergessen habe, der ist, dass ich nie sehe, welcher Tag es ist. Oder genauer, welches Datum. Früher habe ich es gesehen, überall. Wir alle haben es gesehen. Bevor es Computer gab, habe ich täglich fünf oder sechs Faxe von der Arbeit aus verschickt, jedes davon mit Datum versehen. In meinem Büro hing ein Kalender, in tragbarer, den man mit zu Meetings nehmen konnte, und ein Hochglanzfotokalender schmückte meine Küchenwand. Berichtsbegleitschreiben? Vier oder fünf am Tag. Briefe? Einige. Alles brauchte ein Datum. Verzweifelt wollte man, dass die Empfänger von wichtigen Dokumenten wussten, wann man sie verschickt hatte. Ich schrieb diese Begleitschreiben mit der Hand, heftete sie an die Ordner mit den Berichten und rief den Fahrradkurier an. Ich sah zu, wie das Faxgerät am laufenden Band den heißgeliebten Zettel ausspuckte, auf dem stand, „Nachricht versandt", und das Datum. Empfangsdamen, Sekretärinnen, Angestellte der Poststelle auf der ganzen Welt öffneten Umschläge, erduldeten Papierschnitte und stempelten sorgfältig das Datum auf jeden Brief, sogar auf die Werbepost. Im unwahrscheinlichen Falle, dass der Tag verging, ohne dass ich etwas faxte oder einen Brief schrieb, stellte ich wahrscheinlich einen Scheck aus. Und weil ich ständig das Datum sah, konnte ich die erste Zeile blitzschnell ausfüllen: Datum. Beim Einkaufen, um Rechnungen zu bezahlen und für die Reinigung schrieb man Schecks. Es gab sogar ‚Barschecks', die man sich von den Bankangestellten auszahlen ließ. Weil ich jetzt zu selten Schecks schreibe, schwebt mein Stift immer ein paar Sekunden über dieser ersten leeren Zeile, und ich muss überlegen, welches Datum wir haben. Das Datum steht unten rechts auf dem Computerbildschirm und macht kühn auf allen Handydisplays auf sich aufmerksam. Aber wir sehen es nicht. Heutzutage sehen wir die Uhrzeit, denn unsere Tage sind zu Minuten zusammengeschrumpft. Am Abend des neunundachtzigsten Geburtstags meines Vaters bemerkte ich mein Versehen. Als ich um zehn im Bett lag, musste ich eine Entscheidung treffen. Anrufen und ihn aufwecken und den Tag ehren, oder mich am nächsten Tag reumütig entschuldigen. Ich entschied mich für letzteres, denn er ist neunundachtzig und braucht seinen Schlaf, und nächtliche Anrufe können besorgniserregend sein. Vater hat am nächsten Morgen meine Entschuldigung angenommen, aber ich spürte, wie seine eigentlich noch starke Stimme leicht stockte. Hätte er neben mir gestanden, die Röte im Gesicht hätte meine Demütigung verraten. Sein Geburtstag ist jetzt eine Meeting-Erinnerung in Großbuchstaben in meinem Outlook-Kalender, zwei Tage vor seinem Geburtstag (um die Karte rechtzeitig abzuschicken), einen Tag vorher (nur zur Sicherheit), und am eigentlichen Tag. Vielleicht fahre ich nächstes Jahr einfach die hundertachtzig Meilen und besuche ihn.

NICOLAS POYNTER |

poof

Mr. Santiago died last week, heart attack during fourth hour. The girls screamed so loud I heard them down in the gym. He had been losing it for some time, yelling at us for not paying attention, clutching his chest. His death surprises no one.

"I used to be just like you idiots," he told us that day. "I used to think I knew everything too."

I asked him what he meant, after the bell, kids were pushing past me and flooding out into the hall, maybe twenty or thirty minutes before I would hear the screams, basketballs would be raining down.

"I only know one thing now." He said. "Poof... That's all." And his hand had formed into a claw, his lungs exhaled a faint, wheezing, defeated sound.

Poof.

This time thing; it's not everything it seems to be.

Mr. Santiago taught me Einstein and how to build the atomic bomb. And when I heard Einstein thought he was a loser, I thought about making bombs. And when I heard he flunked math, I thought about revolution. I thought about him, the drop-out, throwing ideas around like hand grenades, and then maybe those ideas traveled for a hundred years and blew up the only wal-mart in town. I watched the explosion, all that cheap crap I really thought I needed vanishing from both time and space, burning all the way to the ground.

Poof.

Cops are trying to pin that one on me.

The principal said we must have the pep assemblies, even though we are all drowned out by the still-fresh screams from Mr. Santiago's classroom echoing off the matted walls. Wasted, heavy, hooded sweatshirt, headphones to a radio that will no longer play. I'm some peach-fuzzed refugee. The principal lurks below, cops at each side, striding fast out into the middle of the hardwood floor. Cold fingers wrap around my throat. He points right at me and I think I can just read his lips, shoot that motherfucker, so I start to run. But they tackle me like Jesus before I can get to the door.

No, this was never going to be a suicide note.

Those jokers pull me out of there the long way, by my feet, my sweatshirt dusting a stripe right down the middle of the court. They say they got evidence and are going to lock me up forever. I just stare at the faces as I slide by, all those kids looking down at me, thinking I'm stupid, thinking I'm ugly, thinking I'm a lost cause. "I used to be just like you idiots," I yell at them. "I used to think I knew everything too!" Then poof, I'm out of there forever, the cheerleaders line up and applaud.

RICHARD O'CONNELL |

fractals

Huidobro

In Chile there are only two directions:
North and South. One bird: the condor.
Huidobro invented the Andes.

Savannah

The name is a song. Home of Johnny
Mercer and Flannery O'Connor.
Antebellum still. In Savannah there is no
such thing as a "rush hour."

Rattler

There is a type of man who must rattle
and read The Financial Times on the
beach. That man is my enemy.

Mr. Dodgson (Lewis Carroll)

The fact that he liked to photograph little
girls in the buff did not banish him from
the best households in England. That
happy isle. Where eccentricity is still
expected and respected.

Martial

No poet is so identified with his genre. To
this day Martial and epigram are
synonymous . In a sense they invented
each other. Too one-dimensional?
Perhaps.But what a welter of life laid bare
by that scalpel.

Obit: Patrice Cobb-Cooper

The dowager empress of the Irish Society
of Boca Raton dominated all with her
loud, insolent, rasping voice. Always
larger than life and in control. When one
of her wealthy husbands died in Ireland
laughing and his grown up "children"
objected to burying him in Europe, she
shipped him home to them in Chicago
C.O.D. Her quiet, self-effacing demise left
stuffy Boca greatly diminished.

Lizbeth Scott

I was too young to appreciate the movie
star's smoky, sultry style. When asked to
obtain her
signature for a Chesterfield advertising
poster over at the Plaza by my ad agency,
I declined because it was getting late and I
was in a hurry to get home. To the Bronx!

Edward G. Robinson

Dynamic and explosive in whatever role
he undertook. I'd give anything to know
what he whispered into Lauren Bacall's
ear in Key Largo. From her shocked,
outraged reaction I'm sure of one thing: it
was not in the script.

Bogart

His edgy, high-voltage performance in
The Maltese Falcon has probably never
been equaled. A peculiar electrical
intensity conveyed through his glistening
eyes.

Jack Palance

The snakelike, sexually suggestive way he
slides off a horse in Shane is one of the
unforgettable moments in film, wryly
counterpointed by Ladd's "He ain't no
cowpoke."

Hitchcock

Knew a lot about the hidden, excremental
character of murder. Watch, for example,
the raising of the mud-caked submerged
death car at the end of Psycho.

Benny Hill

Despite an obvious debt to Red Skelton,
one of our most original comics. The

danse macabre striptease sequence in which he even divests himself of his skeleton is a surrealist masterpiece.

Lee Marvin
The voice alone was worth the price of admission.

Retirement
Better to die in harness than to amble off to the glue factory simply because you have nothing better to do. Most of us need the routine of work if only to appreciate leisure.

Carnival
"But everything is sexual," the Brazilian poet exclaimed, wiping the sweat rolling down his brown flabby face, his black eyes bulging behind thick glasses like some incredible nocturnal insect.

William Carlos Williams
Our Theocritus of smoke stacks. inventor of the Industrial Idyll, Poetry depicting those wretched stretches of weeds, broken glass strewn backyards, clapboard houses, dumps, moribund hospitals. abandoned factories, warehouses, etc. All the detritus of the broken, toxic, disconnected waste lands of North Jersey.

Jimmy Doolittle
His daring carrier raid on Tokyo inflicted negligible military damage, but the damage to Japanese pride precipitated the pivotal battle of Midway. In war as in everything else the full impact of events is not always immediately apparent.

Deanna Durbin
While still in uniform I had the privilege of escorting the beautiful famous singer to the Monte Carlo Ballet in Monaco. Why

she selected an anonymous American sailor to accompany her, I'll never know. We were given choice seats.

Virgil
That pious prick. Aeneas. Always "on duty."

W. C. Fields
His consummate inability to get himself unglued probably had its origin in the sticky, gluon nature of his native Philadelphia.

Baseball
Complex as chess. The essence of concentration and confrontation. A game of vectors and velocities.

Flying Down to Rio
An aerial delight, The bare-breasted show girls riding the wings of biplanes doing acrobatics over Rio is a wonderful futuristic fusion of sexual/mechanical energy.

Valle de los Caidos (Valley of the Fallen)
Located outside Madrid in high, cool, pine-scented air: Franco's mountain monument dedicated to the dead of the Spanish Civil War. More like the Holland Tunnel than a tomb or church. Still less a cathedral. Eternally leaking . . . or is it the tears of those stone Angels dressed as aviators?

Jimmy Stewart
He never played the bad guy. That was not to his credit, though he did write a few good poems.

c

Whether looking at the stars or each other, all we can perceive is the past whether in light years or nano-seconds. In a real sense once we accept the speed of light as an absolute, only the past exists.

Richard Feynman

The Peter Pan of quantum physics never lost touch with the element of play central to his remarkable work.

Mnemosyne

Mother of the Muses. Apparently it is the idiosyncratic constructs of memory that best define us as a species. Memory is not a given or a result but a unique artifact made in the here and now.

MacArthur

My father never forgave him for firing on the WW I bonus marchers in Washington. He never seemed to miss a photo opportunity. How many times have we seen it-the picture of MacArthur wading ashore, getting his pressed pants wet "returning". Or as I heard a bitter Marine say, "Yes, MacArthur took the Philippines/ with the help of God and a few Marines."

Manuel Bandeira

When I met the great patriarch of modern Brazilian poetry in his apartment near the Santos Dumont Airport in Rio I thought he resembled a small carved mahogany idol from the Amazon jungle. He totally surprised me by reciting one of my poems in flawless English.

Franz K.

Our Ovid of the quotidian. Gregor, after being turned into an insect, still tries to go to work. Much like those old Wolf Man movies in which Lon Chaney Jr., dressed in a clean white shirt and tie and determined to be ordinary, mournfully notices tufts of hair erupting on his hands.

Patrick McGoohan

Too bad they didn't award him a retro Oscar for his remarkable work in the Secret Agent television series back in the 60s. Photographed against the bleak chiaroscuro of cold war Europe, his blend of good looks, technical know how and icy intelligence made him the perfectly believable Secret Agent.

JFK

When I first saw him and Jackie at the National Art Gallery he was still the junior senator from Massachusetts-taller and leaner than I expected-pointedly ignored by the Washington crowd. I turned to Pierre Emmanuel and said, "He'll be president." "He'll never get elected with a wife like that," Pierre dryly replied, implying that America would never accept a chic First Lady.

Wilde in the Wild West

What a wild madcap merry musical it would make- Oscar Wilde entertaining gold miners in Colorado during the time of Jesse James.

The Pencil

Still the primary tool of philosophers and poets. Hard to find one these days. I remember when they used to be peddled on large trays by blind beggars in the subway. Of course you were not supposed to ever actually buy one.

The Thimble

Encapsulates the female mystique: smooth, ovaled, sieved, steel.

John Bell

His Theorem suggests that we inhabit a ghostly quantum cosmos where everything is magically interconnected and affected by everything else in unimaginable ways. A possibility: instantaneous telepathy under the imprimatur of Pa Bell.

Einstein

Heisenberg's Uncertainty Principle did not sit well with his post-Newtonian postulates. Contrary to his own earlier quantum discoveries, he refused to accept the idea of a chancy, wild card universe. God does not play dice! You can almost hear him. From the stars.

Elizabeth Bishop

We spent an afternoon in her patron's lavish mountain mansion in Petropolis discussing Robert Lowell's poetry. I remember complaining about Lowell's harping on being a Lowell in Life Studies and her prim reply, "Well, after all he is a Lowell."

Jack Benny

Probably our finest, most sophisticated comedian: the ultimate straight man. Master of the serial joke and minimalist humor.

Othello

How quickly his Venetian veneer wears off! He speaks and behaves like an Oriental potentate. Like Mohammed, he suffers from epilepsy. By Islamic law the punishment for adultery is death. Othello is an infidel.

Hamlet & Hamburger

Orson Welles observed that in Hamlet Shakespeare tried to write a tragedy about a genius and that he never made that mistake again. I once asked a writing class to imagine how Hamlet would order a hamburger. One student wrote a dissertation.

Gide

The way out of the Labyrinth is the way in. At the center of the maze you must meet and murder your Minotaur.

Hiroshima

More horrific than those grotesque, lifelike plaster cast moulds of Pompeii's suffocated victims: the shadows of the living imprinted on a wall remnant by the blinding, incinerating flash of the A-bomb.

November 22, 1963

We had just finished discussing Crime and Punishment when I noticed a commotion outside the classroom building. People were running in different directions across the campus. I looked out the ground-floor window toward the women's dormitory where something caught my eye. From one of the windows hung a white towel, printed in large letters in bright lipstick KENNEDY DEAD.

J. Robert Oppenheimer

A crucial figure in the full sense of the word. A free thinking poet and brilliant physicist, he embodied all the contradictions of the age. Probably the only scientist at Los Alamos who fully grasped the momentous nature of what they euphemistically called 'the gadget."

RITA D. COSTELLO |

paper   scissors   rock: september 11th, 2001

After all this, finally it sinks in why paper
wins the game. The frail   slips of
nothing
float and coil at the edge of billows,
rolling under and
resurfacing until finally settling last   on
dust
that was stone and shelter, on glass now
returned to its
former life as sand, steel shredded or
splayed in hollow

frames that play with the light in urban
pretension
to Golgotha. It always ends in damaged
symbols and
Middle Eastern land, doesn't it? The
markets closed as
if Christ had entered the temple again,
berating the callousness
of coins or fixed   the cross forever with
marred spikes
driven through crumpled bodies, both
falling
and raised skyward in the awkward light
that survives

in devastation. In strange moments of
glancing
upward, at once expecting and knowing
there will be
no distant planes. On the right side of the
Trade Center the sun
still shines, in places   even puncturing
the pumice smoke
only moments ago contouring its rays in a
river careening

lava-like through crevices,
formerly   streets and

sidewalks. The rest of us stuck to
televisions, struck
by sick jealousy for those so close to
dissatisfaction
made physical; powerful enough to admit
a real language, a
punctuation of *fucks* and *fucker* to our
national dialogue,
on daytime t.v. Because, who   could
pretend to protect us, as
tidal waves foam through the alleys of
Manhattan, cleansing
and coating in debris. Because paper
always   covers rock.

discovering resonance
    —for Jesse

fuck the drumroll   this is the beat of life
tonguing the Ritalin to a sour face
just to enable a smile
the rhythm   of the skateboard's wheels
clacking the city cement   is music
the buses and braking and business   of
High St.
is beautiful   he says
you just have to learn to hear it   to fall in love

smoking a bowl behind the high school
gym
was the only way he could make it this
still   this long
but there's nothing in *this* for him   any
longer:

I tell you   in fourth grade
she tied me down to the desk
with my own leather belt
and I waited so long
to be let up again

he'll learn it   by living it
with sticks   on skins
life and love   and the streets
that leave Virginia
for people that move with real music

morning: after work   he speaks with
pride that's overwhelming
swaying out the story of his father   to a
soft Radiohead song
about plastic
played loud on the stereo
downstairs   his father in federal prison
getting his degree   getting out
getting on with his life   as an English
teacher

fuck the drumroll   he says
this isn't an introduction   this is a drum
this is the way   skin is supposed to sound
when you beat on it

RYAN NEGRINI |

noah

Noah was normal and regular and plain,
But he was clever and had a magnificent
brain.

He would ride with the neighbors to
school each day
And during his recess he liked to play.

He liked to climb trees and he liked to
play ball.
He could run like the rest and like them
he would fall.

But today, he was out with his friends
riding trikes
And they whispered the secret of who
they "like liked."

Hayden liked Mary and Mary liked Clark,
But Noah liked Hayden and the other
boys barked.

"You can't like a boy! Pick a girl that you
know!"
And Noah just said, "I can't and I won't."

He liked the way Hayden was ever so
smart,
And enjoyed playing tag with him in the
school yard

They got along best when they danced in
the trees,
And laughed as the people below picked
off leaves.

During church service they would both
sing and clap,

And they slept near each other when it
was time for a nap

They were ordinary boys, no one better
than the rest,
But equal in all ways, the way it was best.

maybe some hope

For a kid it's not hard to just run away,
Turn the block, cross the street, hop on
the subway.
But us? We have jobs, kids, loans and
connections
No room for differences, no free love, no
affections

Shouting for skeletons face down in
closets,
Whispers about people who got lost
inside it.
Then again, the closet's a safe place to be,
When the planet is piping hot with
disease.

The illness can't get to minds covered in
fear
You quest out the closet and get called a
queer
Now you're out trying to get passed the
pits,
Find somewhere to fit, like a puzzle piece,
and sit.

You're tired and just need some time to
think,
And in the moment you blink, you've
been sent to the brink.
Mass destruction, denial, abuse, and pure
hate,
But you don't dictate to what they
masturbate.

They say you're not equal, whose rights
do you tote?
So the rest of us send love and maybe
some hope.
Why give in to the pressure of hateful
infections?
Be proud of your differences, free love
and affections.

words like empty pockets

We sit here silent, almost weeping
Shouting, Screaming. Only peeping
Thoughts long thought by many thinkers
Spineless sinners, Science bringers
Something's heavy in the air
Always in this house so bare.

Waiting, listening, shaking, nodding
Suddenly again I'm trodden
Can the seers mum the prophet
Profit prophets won't allow it
Is a heartbeat really there?
Always in this house so bare.

Along comes creeping now and then,
Some skin and teeth to choke the hen
And clucking then was all I heard
Not elephant, but fucking bird.
Now settled with a stringent glare
Always in this house so bare.

The cotton soft of empty pockets
Breaks not prophets golden lockets,
But singing high as birdies do
Gives equal voice to those who stew
No longer will they grin and bear
Never in this house so bare.

SAÏDEH PAKRAVAN |

abbie hoffman is dead

My nerves are bad tonight, yes bad. (T.S. Eliot)

They've been bad all week. The world pushes at me harder than it has in a while. War and desolation and my own troubles filtered through a murky pane of exhaustion, absent-minded motions, out-of-touch with myself as ageing, this cascade of others pouring ice on a body and a head that long for night.

Growing up, I pranced about in a 3-D world, most assuredly wearing the tranquil smile of Samoans living on this globe of green forests and blue seas, mighty icebergs, animals not threatened by extinction cuddling their young, birds flying above in migrations that we could follow when we shielded our eyes and threw our heads back far enough.

Bad things did happen, even back then. We never thought of the world as paradise—at a young age we had been taught that suffering was part and parcel of life, as were starvation, wars, and nightmares. After all, we'd forfeited our right to paradise long ago, hadn't we? God, as vengeful then as now, applied the one-strike-and-you're-out rule. You took a bite from which apple? Get out, get out now! Sweat and tears will be your lot for as long as I decide to allow your species to exist.

Yes, bad things did happen. An earthquake in Iran killed twenty-five thousand people. Twenty-five thousand. The awful number had the world in tears.

Aid streamed in from everywhere, the rubble was cleared, houses rebuilt. Other bad things happened— planes tumbled down from the sky, young people were killed in car crashes. But incidents fell at great intervals, each one stood out, singular, unique in the horror it evoked. I cried my eyes out every time. But as elastic as my youth made me, I jumped right back to top form. Then the years passed, the world moved to its present fast track, and I started running out of breath. World population grew exponentially. Four, five, six, seven billion, from the three we had always heard there were, so statistics changed in every way. Numbers unheard of a decade before became the norm as people fell, victims of this or that wild man, this or that god gone berserk, catastrophes, killer waves, the earth splitting open and swallowing whole civilizations, tribesmen with machetes. Every war, every famine, every pestilence, killed tens, hundreds of thousands. Mass murderers, bloodied up to their eyes, cut up limbs and torsos in a paroxysm of glee, religious fanatics blew themselves and others up, eyes looked up from deep sockets as sunken and questioning as those of camp survivors but in different faces. The age, the pleated skins, the color, the gender, jump at us on our search engine screen, on National Geographic covers, on the railings of the Luxembourg Garden.

A few years back, the Burmese junta stole the food sent by the world to help the starving hordes victims of Hurricane Nargis, an earthquake killed countless Chinese, the horrors of the Bush administration kept coming to light in numbing accounts of torture, rendition, drugging of helpless illegals, destruction of the environment.

In "Steal this movie" on Abbie Hoffman, we are reminded that he killed himself, and wasn't that a sad day. There have been other good people before and since. Another movie is about the Englishman who for thirty years pushed for the abolition of the slave trade before he succeeded, and then there's the story of the German woman who died a few months ago. She had saved 2,500 children from the Varsaw ghetto, smuggled them out patiently, one by one, starting in 1939, envisioning full well the horror about to be unleashed and that most people said they could never have imagined.

And still people mutter, how could we know this or that and still the world shies away from seeing how far it's gone and still I cry and still the world pursues jug jug to dirty ears.

Abbie Hoffman is dead. Where in the world would people like that stand, where do they hide these days, the bearers of sustainable passion, of never-ending anger, of absurd outbursts, the carriers of fires that keep burning when all the fuel is gone?

The world has kept on turning. A quarter century later, the Burmese military can join hands with God to swat a million people who drifted with swollen bellies on the Irrawaddy Delta, ungainly water lilies floating among the debris washed here and there on the sluggish waves then, as an afterthought, decorating the carcasses on the bank where sharp-eyed carrions cannot believe their luck.

Meanwhile in a distant palace a general undoes his armored vest to allow his full belly to expand. He burps and through his empty mind passes no thought of those drifting bodies nor of the tens of thousands crushed by hunger, sorrow, and pelting rain. Instead, sated after his meal, he vaguely surveys mentally the accumulated riches sent by a grieving world, signals for his plate to be removed, unwary of the waiter who approaches, thick kitchen chopper in hand, and splits open his skull, the waiter who has lost eleven family members in the Delta, who will avenge them so their souls can float away in peace, who no longer minds paying the price.

NICHOLAS KOMODORE |

Manifold

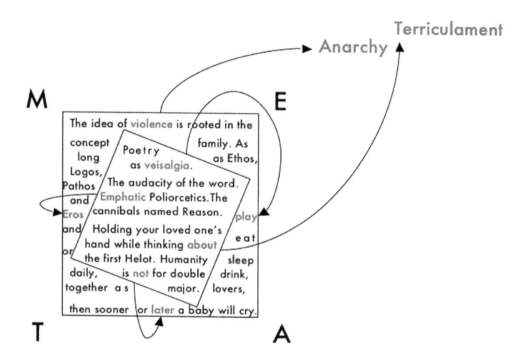

SAM SMITH |

sex with the famous

Academics can't come across the ordinary
without seeking some metaphorical
significance.
And no matter how often
I tell myself to speak the unspeakable,
print the unprintable, to spit on all
their bibles and flags, here I am again
trapped by my own politeness, wearing
the forbearing smile that has heard
these stories before; and I wait to hear
them out again. . . .
Nothing-much theories,
one shot at making a self interesting:
all, though, are but interpretations
of others' lives. . . .

Sex mit Berühmtheiten

Akademiker können auf nichts
Gewöhnliches stoßen, immer suchen sie
einen metaphorischen
Sinn.
Und egal wie oft
ich mich zwinge, das Unsagbare zu sagen,
das Undruckbare zu drucken, Spucke auf
all ihre
Bibeln und Flaggen zu schmieren, ich bin
wieder
gefangen in meiner eigenen Höflichkeit,
trage
das wissende Lächeln, das diese
Geschichten schon mal gehört hat; und
ich lasse
sie wieder ausreden. . . .
Nichts-sagende Theorien,
eine einzige Chance, ein Ich interessant zu
machen:

alles, jedoch, ist nichts als Interpretation
des Lebens anderer. . . .

i am english

1)

If aired here the profoundest thoughts get
mocked, not expounded upon, not
challenged, the holder more likely sneered
at - with that hooded eye and leaning
away lip lift that the stupid and the
uneducated English cultivate.

In the suburban sprawl that is England
today public debate there is none, the
deepest of feelings get expressed only in
the tiredest of sentiments or the coarsest
of oaths. In this prison of national vanity,
a country under the control of the lowest
common denominator - violence,
tribalism, self-centredness - the English
underclass seen now as a low snivelling
breed, these the punished poor are feared
more than the feted rich.

Still our establishment, governments so
corrupt they don't know they're corrupt,
prefer to persuade by prejudice than to act
on principle, than to convince by reason,
so they revert to clumsy behaviourism,
war their one common purpose. When
they can find no enemy beyond our
borders the English mind-set seeks only
to gain advantage over their fellow
citizens. Or English holidaymakers return
from their ghetto tourism to complain of
appalling service.

With reaction against English snobbery-
pretending-artistic-sensitivity having led
to the shockjock nonsense of English art -
blind dwarves on the shoulders of giants.
If England were to possess an active

intelligentsia so offended, so slighted would the rest feel, secure in their self-cultivated ignorance, they would gleefully reinstate public executions.

2)

In this world I have lived among all that other men have made. I have looked down the iron sides of ships to petrol-sheened dockwater, driven cars in among other cars, eaten biscuits baked in other countries, lost myself in landscapes and books made by the long dead....

In this world I have lived according to, at different times, various of other men's rules. I have tried to be as others. But a people, as a people, to become a people, have to get marched off to war. At least once. And I have never found a war worth fighting, have suspected every offer of friendship, have refused to be trapped by any tribe. I don't like the English.

In this world I have lived my adult life as a writer, and now - nearing the end of this life - I find that I have given all those years up to a pointless exercise. Should you be tempted to do the same it is probably best that you first accept that no one anywhere cares about you and what you do. No one really cares. Not about what you might think. Not about what you might say, unless you break their rules. English individuals just want to get on with their own lives. At best the million words I've written have been a mild diversion, most likely an irrelevance. I am English.

to fossilise v.t.

Take a fresh body
flat as an empty pocket

and in its debt-cancelling departure
put stained coppers on what were the
eyes.

Ask if
a burial chamber would have offered

the comfort of company to them living,
or would their preference have been

for a single company
egotistical one-name grave?

Whether or not
to add an urn?

Feel your entire alive being
lightened by a decision made,

leave the result for the finding of
an as yet unborn archeologist.

where

window walls
are as unflattering as
bright-lit mirrors made-lame
beggars clutch at the ankles of self-
fashioning aesthetes and hedge fund usury
and electronic alchemy seed the future
with disgust

MAKINGS OF MANIAC: SAM WAINWRIGHT & DAN WELSH |

the reified concepts conferring meaning upon the meaningless and some of the impacts caused (in an admittedly one-sided presentation of opinion)

(1. Money)

A divisive conception that made up rich and poor, [ ] Could've all been equalish but now some have so much more, [ ] Little bits of nowt at all that are desperately clung onto, [ ] Even though we all accept it has no intrinsic value, [ ] Yet still read the rich list in The Times as if a measurement of power, [ ] Veneration for mostly wealth through birth leaves me fucking sour, [ ] To justify its own continuance, masquerades as the 'great allower', [ ] But I don't need a credit card to enjoy an April Shower, [ ] I want to live in a world without a fee to not go hungry, [ ] The dilemma posed, I'm sunk in stupor, I want folk to do it for me. [ ]

(2. Time)

I don't need to know what time it is, and I'd rather it that way [ ] Organised around a clock in't the nicest way to live the day, [ ] Imprisoning to others' rule, tick-tock be your sedation, [ ] The freedom quelling wall-eye's gaze enforces your deflation, [ ] Yet clocks aren't real they're just made up to numericise the hours, [ ] But following their stringent rule makes chains to disempower, [ ] Clocks and Calendars aren't the actual problem just the way they're used, [ ] The sheer detest of the working week can give sufficient clues, [ ] Time is real just not the names, and time will pass you by, [ ] But it's not entirely necessary to know if it's February or July. [ ]

(3. Nations and borders)

Nations states are just made up, we drew the borders on, [ ] My cliché cynicism suspects by an upper echelon, [ ] They monopolise violence, but I belong to no one but mi mam, [ ] But sketchmarks in cartography argue I'm tied unto this land, [ ] I like it yeh, but if I dint, it's my freedom to leave, [ ] For where I do without harassment that a passport be unsheathed, [ ] Cause no one owns the world, and you can't own men or land, [ ] Except like before where I said I'm owned by mi mam, [ ] Banging pegs in the ground dun't mean a thing, it dun't make it really yours, [ ] And tell me I can't walk somewhere I'll fight it teeth and claws.

(4.Culture)

It's debatable to say race in't real cause I can see some difference, [ ] But cause someone's brown and someone's not in't enough to decry coexistence, [ ] So cultural differences are proffered but that dunt justify it either, [ ] Cause culture dunt exist in a vacuum and differences impact on each other, [ ] And culture isn't providence but occurs through circumstances, [ ] Summat created so haphazardly can't claim to have the answers, [ ] Nor is it so static but is always rearranging, [ ] So stop being so fucking racist it dun't matter if it's changing.

(5.Names and Language)

I don't espouse all not natural is by
default a bad idea, [ ] If we hadn't
invented Names then we'd all be shouting
'ere', 'you', [ ] 'the fat one, black one,
thin one, white one, [ ] ugly, smelly,
filthy, boring but I still might one', [ ]
And language too is all made up but still
has done us good, [ ] Else
communication reduces to non-descript
groan, and thud [ ] Of something thrown
in the aim of winning your merely sensory
attention, [ ] So some of the things that
weren't here first have turned
out good inventions, [ ] But
aforementioned stuff's mostly bad, or at
least has become so, [ ] Some seem of
noble origin, it's just what they've been
turned into, [ ] The harms outweigh
initial optimism when hijacked by powers
that be, [ ] But no doubt I'll just sit and
wait for someone else to change it for me.

die vergegenständlichten Konzepte, die dem Bedeutungslosen Bedeutung geben, und einige ihrer Auswirkungen (in einer zugegeben einseitigen Meinungsdarlegung)

(1. Geld)

Die verschiedenen Meinungen von arm
und reich, [ ] Hätten sich einigen
können, doch jetzt ist vieles ungleich, [ ]
An kleine Stücke Nix wird sich
verzweifelt geklammert, [ ] Obwohl
sonst doch niemand Papierscheine
sammelt, [ ] Die Times listet Reiche auf
und verteilt so Macht, [ ] Verehrung von

reich Geborenen, dass ich nicht lach', [ ]
Eine gütige Maske ermöglicht das immer
weiter, [ ]
Doch keine Kreditkarte macht das Wetter
heiter, [ ] Ich will keine Gebühr für
Essen im Magen, [ ]
Das Dilemma ist da, jetzt müsst ihr was
sagen.

(2. Zeit)

Wie spät es ist, das weiß ich nicht, so soll
es von mir aus auch sein, [ ] Rund um
die Uhr organisiert zu sein, beengt mich
und macht mich ganz klein, [ ] Gefangen
in den Regeln Fremder, das tick-tack
betäubt dich fast ganz, [ ] Der schielende
Blick, der deine Freiheit unterdrückt,
führt dich im tödlichen Tanz, [ ] Uhren
sind nur erfunden um Stunden zu
strukturieren, [ ] Und ihr Regiment
nimmt dich gefangen und du musst
kapitulieren, [ ] Kalender und Uhren sind
nicht, was mich stört, sondern nur, wie ihr
sie verehrt, [ ] Dass euch ein jeder
Montagmorgen mit seiner Grauheit nicht
bekehrt, [ ] die Zeit ist realer als die
Namen die wir ihr geben, und Zeit wird
weitergeh'n, [ ] Dazu ist es nicht
unbedingt notwendig, die Worte Juli oder
Februar zu seh'n.

(3. Länder und Grenzen)

Nationen sind Erfindungen, die Grenzen
nur gemalt, [ ] Und zynisch wer da denkt,
das wird mit einer Hierarchie bezahlt, [ ]
Sie nutzen Gewalt, aber ich gehöre
niemandem als meiner Mama, [ ] Doch
Kritzeleien in der Kartographie sollen mich
binden an dieses Land, [ ] Ich mag es hier,
ja, doch wollte ich weg, dann wäre ich nicht
länger frei, [ ] Ein Pass bindet fest, wo
könnte ich hin, ohne dass man mich hier

hält, [ ] Die Welt gehört keinem, nicht
Mensch oder Land, [ ] Ich gehöre
niemandem außer meiner Mama, [ ] Pfähle
im Boden bedeuten nichts, sie machen es
nicht zu deinem, [ ] Und wenn du mich
hältst, bekämpfe ich dich, mit allem, mit
Armen und Beinen.

(4. Kultur)

Man kann sich streiten, ob es Rassen so
gibt, die Unterschiede sind gegeben, [ ]
Doch auch wenn man braun ist und
jemand ist's nicht, kann man miteinander
leben, [ ] Die Unterschiede in der Kultur
sind nicht Grund genug so zu trennen, [ ]
Kultur existiert nicht im Vakuum, nur im
Vergleich
kann man etwas ‚anders' nennen, [ ] Und
Kultur ist nicht vorbestimmt, sondern
allein durch
Umstände ist sie so, [ ] Was Willkür
geschaffen, kann nicht vorschreiben, die
Antwort sei so oder so, [ ] Auch statisch
ist sie keinesfalls, sondern ändert sich fast
jeden Tag, [ ] Also sei kein verdammter
Rassist, nur weil du Veränderung nicht
magst.

(5. Namen und Sprache)

Ich behaupte nicht, alles Unnatürliche sei
schlecht, [ ] Ohne Namen, wären wir alle
‚hey' und ‚du'
[ ] ‚der Fette, der Schwarze, der Dünne,
oder der Weiße, [ ] Würden hässlich,
stinkend, dreckig oder langweilig' heißen,
[ ] Auch Sprache ist eine Erfindung von
uns, und trotzdem hat sie geholfen, [ ]
Nicht nur mit Ächzen zu kommunizieren
und mit Fäusten unbeholfen [ ] Zu
schlagen und so die Aufmerksamkeit der
Sinne zu bekommen, [ ] Manche Dinge,
die es nicht immer gab, sind dennoch gut

geworden, [ ] Doch das Zeug, von dem
ich vorhin sprach, ist schlecht oder wurd's
gemacht, [ ]
Obwohl es einen edlen Ursprung hat, ist
es jetzt nur noch zu verachten, [ ] Sein
Schaden wiegt schwerer als jede gute
Absicht, wenn Herrscher sich ihm
annehmen, [ ] Also zweifle ich, sitze und
warte darauf, dass jemand das für mich
angeht.

there's no such thing as (the big) society: the lady's not for learning

All simple displays of binary questions,
Playing fools with dichotomous face value
opinions,
Not mould-of-Marx-hardened
revolutionaries,
Nor were they cold calculated
mercenaries,
Don't condemn or support blindly and
outright,
Lots were just dickheads going out for the
fight,
Not in reaction to that man getting killed,
But to get a new mac without being billed,
Cause otherwise they couldn't afford it,
Cause the rich have the money and a
penchant for hoarding,
But this kind of behaviour is not the
solution,
Firebombing Greggs won't bring
revolution,

With words in their mouths, styled
excuses from lawyers,
Most didn't go out cause they can't find
employers,
And it's not about having a lack of youth
centres,
Rationality leaves, and bullshit enters,

Most couldn't express the reason they
riot,
With brains being scrambled by
poisonous diet,
Cause it's all they can afford, and they
hadn't been taught,
The value of food for coherent thought,
And that's not the only thing not being
shown,
So in that respect they didn't cast the first
stone,
Whilst the trigger was state endorsed
murder,
The coverage developed attention deficit
disorder,
And forgot MP expenses is privileged
looting,
And neglect to recall the aforementioned
police shooting,
Or draw a parallel with the Bullingdon
Club,
Because apparently it's different if you
have red or blue blood,
And this status quo keeps you from
reaching the top,
So why the fuck not destroy a brand name
shoe shop?

Because it's better to riot than pathetically
protest,
Not much more useless than ordered
unrest,
Like begging your master with please,
please, please,
I'd rather die on my feet than get down
on my knees,
To wait in neat lines to 'give you a voice',
May make yourself heard but still leaves
them the choice,
To disregard you because they have the
power,
But they only have that because you allow
it,

But if we war-cry 'fuck off', clenched fist,
bared teeth,
There's nowt they can do because their
power is belief,
In their power to which we passively
comply,
So they revel in rich reverence and we
barely scrape by,
So those in the riots weren't the morally
spent,
Cause we're only the products of our
environment,
Yet they're surprised when the rats they
breed bite them back,
When you're tormented enough your last
choice is attack,
And then mass produce dogs but
complain at dogshit,
But then just go on and step over it,
And don't address the root cause, namely
inequality,
And expect people to put up with
enforced poverty,
And sing a long to their tune 'cause it's
best for us all',
I can't fucking wait for the day that they
fall,
And the riots have shown they don't
stand a chance,
They can build their own disco but they
can't make us dance,
Why should we listen to anything they
say,
When we eat dirt for the privileged day
after day,
Doing jobs that we hate for the tens and
the fives,
That directly lead to having no stake in
our lives,
There are no benefits to us in all their talk
of 'progress',
As all outside The City ends up with less,
'But we're all in this together, we're the
same you and me,

Oh and before I forget we've shut your library',

So we work for their money and get enough for the day,
And swallow the medicine that 'it must be this way',
Cause without a big Tesco the sun wouldn't shine,
And without a new macbook my health will decline,
Well I'd rather 40 years happy than a century enslaved,
But the price for long life is my freedom is waived,
So shelves are stacked but I don't care if they're clear,
Cause if no one did that we'd still all be here,
Food would still taste, and the grass would still grow,
Life does not care if the economy is slow,
Yet we are all made slaves to this grotesque fallacy,
And expect to be saved through makeshift social policy,
So there's only one option to make your point known,
That the world is not theirs and we're not backing down,
Yet the civil unrest was no conscious political action,
It was born from inarticulate dissatisfaction,
Cause most were deprived of the tools to express,
Or understand their frustrations or root of distress,
At being excluded and having their lives removed,
All so a few cunts lives are improved,
The point of being alive has been taken away,

To pursue your own happiness and live in each day,
And to go out and experience Earth's rich buffet,
But you can't do that now cause it's a workday,
So why should I uphold their hegemony,
When it appears not to even fucking notice me,
So I can't condemn anyone who sits on the dole,
It's the only way left to loosen the chokehold,
And retain any element of self direction,
But these fine folk are presented as a social infection,

So you can kiss their shoelaces or live under their boot,
Where's the incentive to not riot and loot?
This 'hard work-reward' system doesn't exist,
But fixes false aspirations, but this bit's the twist,
The harder you work the less jobs there are,
So you take something worse to keep up payments for your car,
To get to the job you don't want to buy things you don't need,
And live by a code to which you never agreed,
I had no choice when I was entered into this ludicrous society,
But nor do I have the choice to opt out entirely,
Never was I offered any real variety,
But sewn into a fabric over which I hold no propriety,
I was given a place and expected to sit still,
And restrained to not direct or follow my own natural will,

But it's easy to ignore with all the
processed food in your belly,
And you're too tired from work and X-
Factor's on telly,
And it gets too tough to stand up so you
just go along,
But you'll know it too late when it all goes
Pete Tong

es gibt sie nicht, die (Big) Society: die Dame lernt nicht

Geschlossene Fragen sind leicht und
plausibel,
Für dichotome Narren, die weiß und
schwarz lieben,
Kein Revolutionär aus dem Stoff eines
Marx,
Und auch keine abgerechneten Söldner
waren's,
Verurteilt und helft nicht blind, voll und
ganz,
Die Arschlöcher wollten einfach nur
einen Kampf,
Es ging nicht um Mord, auch wenn der
Mann tot war,
Die wollten nur billig einen neuen
Computer,
Denn eigentlich konnten sie sich den
nicht leisten,
Denn Geld und Kontrolle, das haben die
Reichen,
Aber solch ein Benehmen ist doch keine
Lösung,
Mit Bomben auf Kamps trifft man nicht
nur die Bösen,

Den Mund voller Worte, juristischer
Brocken,
bewegte sich keiner, sie sitzen auf dem
Trockenen,
Und es geht nicht um zu wenige
Jugendvereine,

Der Schwachsinn hält Einzug, Vernunft
bleibt keine,
Oft wussten sie nicht, wogegen sie
kämpfen,
Weil Futter und Fraß ihre Denkfähigkeit
dämpfen
Denn Geld für was Besseres ist oft nicht
vorhanden,
Doch nur richtiges Essen ernährt die
Gedanken,
Und nicht nur davon wussten sie wenig,
Dass sie klein bleiben sollen, dämmert
allmählich,
Der Anlass, ein Mord, den der Staat
unterstützt,
Sogar die Nachrichtensender für
Propaganda benutzt,
Und die dachten nicht dran, dass ihr Geld
ander'n fehlt,
Und die Polizeischießerei wird einfach
verhehlt,
Auch die Kritik an schlagenden
Verbindungen ruht,
Die Dinge laufen wohl anders für Blaues
Blut,
Und genau dieser Zustand treibt dich weg
von der Spitze,
Also warum zur Hölle bleibst du noch
ruhig sitzen?

Denn Aufstand ist besser, als erbärmliche
Demos,
Die kaum etwas bringen und Reformen
geh'n nie los,
Als ob du bitte, bitte bettelst,
Lieber sterbe ich aufrecht, als in euren
Ketten,
Dich ordentlich anzustellen, wo man 'dich
hört',
Gibt dir Chancen zu sprechen, doch sei
nicht empört,
Wenn man dich nicht wahrnimmt, denn
sie haben die Macht,

Doch die haben sie nur, wenn du sie ihnen lässt,
Aber wenn wir brüllen ‚verpisst euch', mit Fäusten,
Dann ist die Macht nix, denn wir lassen uns nicht täuschen
Von ihrer Gewalt, der wir uns passiv ergeben,
Sie baden in Reichtum und wir können kaum leben,
Ein Aufstand macht nicht die Moralischen schwach,
Denn wir sind nur das, was die Welt aus uns macht,
Sie züchten sich Ratten, die sich gegen sie stellen,
Weil sie die ohne andere Auswege quälen,
Und Hunde zu halten, doch Scheiße zu hassen,
Da bleibt ihnen nichts als einen großen Schritt zu machen,
Sie nennen das Elend nicht Ungleichheit,
Und denken, die Leute sind zur Armut bereit,
Und singen gern mit ‚das Beste für alle'
Ich ersehne den Tag, an dem sie endlich fallen,
Und die Aufstände zeigen, sie können nichts machen,
Mit Witzen allein zwingen sie uns nicht zum Lachen,
Warum sollten wir auf ihr Gerede hör'n,
Und uns nicht über ihren Dreck empören,
Jobs machen, die wir hassen für Fünf oder Zehn,
Die sofort wieder zurück an den Arbeitgeber geh'n,
Ihr Fortschritt ist nicht da für unsereins,
Denn irgendein Plus gibt es für uns keins,
„Wir sitzen im selben Boot, wir sind gleich, du und ich,
oh, und bevor ich es vergesse, eine Büchereikriegst du nicht."

Wir verdienen genug Geld für kaum einen Tag,
Und heucheln weiter, dass man das ‚gerne mag',
Denn ohne real,- würde die Sonne nicht scheinen,
Und ohne mein Macbook würd' ich bitterlich weinen,
Lieber zehn Jahre unglücklich als Jahrhunderte versklavt,
Doch der Preis für mein Leben ist Freiheit ist vertan,
Also füll' ich Regale auf, auch wenn's mich nicht interessiert,
Denn auch wenn das niemand täte, wären wir immer noch hier,
Essen würde noch schmecken, und Gras weiter wachsen,
Dem Leben ist es egal, was die Wirtschaft macht,
Und trotzdem hat diese Lüge uns ganz fest im Griff,
Rettet eure notdürftige Sozialpolitik unser Schiff?
Es gibt also nur einen einzigen Weg,
Die Welt gehört allen, und wir gehen nicht weg,
Soziale Unruhen sind noch keine Politik,
Sie geben nur der Unzufriedenheit ihre Sprache zurück,
Denn die meisten sind all ihrer Worte beraubt,
Sehen nur ihren Frust, ihre Angst und den Glauben
Betrogen zu sein, und ihr Leben zu opfern,
Nur weil ein paar Ärsche auf Reichtum hoffen,
Es gibt keinen Grund, immer weiter zu leben,
Jeden Tag zu genießen und nach Glück zu streben,
Und draußen das Buffet der Welt zu erfahren,

Das geht heute nicht, wir müssen ja
arbeiten,
Also warum sollte ich ihre Herrschaft
bedienen,
Wenn sie mir gar nicht nützt, sondern
immer nur ihnen,
Ich kann fast verstehen, dass Menschen
Hartz IV
Dazu nutzen vor diesen Ketten zu fliehen,
Um nur einen Bruchteil ihrer Würde zu
behalten,
Doch heißt es, sie würden eine Krankheit
verbreiten,

Du kannst Füße küssen oder unter ihnen
kriechen,
Gibt es einen Grund, keinen Aufstand zu
verüben?
Das System, das ‚harte Arbeit belohnt',
Existiert nicht, stattdessen bist du es so
gewohnt:
Je mehr Arbeit du machst, desto weniger
ist da,
Also nimmst du was Schlechteres, um
dein Auto zu bezahlen,
Machst Jobs, die du nicht willst, kaufst
Dinge, die du nicht brauchst,
Und lebst nach einem Kodex, dem du gar
nicht vertraust,
Keine Wahl, als ich Teil dieser
Gesellschaft werden musste,
Aber auch keine Wahl, wenn ich jetzt
keine Lust mehr hab,
Eine echte Alternative bekam ich nie zu
Gesicht,
Bin nur Teil eines Gewebes, und finde
mich nicht,
Auf dem mir zugewiesenen Platz soll ich
sitzen bleiben,
Natur oder Wille sollen mich nicht
anderswohin treiben,
Aber das kann man ignorieren, wenn man
sich öfter besäuft,

Und wenn du müde bist von der Arbeit,
und X-Factor läuft,
Und es schwierig ist, aufzustehen, dann
läufst du so mit,
Du weißt erst, dass es zu spät ist, wenn
alles den Bach runtergeht.

SOPHIA COSBY |

may 2, 2011 or sudden and fleeting patriotism

What pride one feels at such glorious
news,
he was offered surrender, but he refused.
So our warriors, famously ready and
armed,
eliminated the man who caused
unforgivable harm.
And thus heartening cheers roamed the
streets,
the triumphant cry of a nation whose foe
is beat.
A unified people, patriotic and loud;
dare anyone else to mess with this crowd.
And avenged are the souls and the hearts
dyed blue,
but will a new faith in America keep those
hearts true?

Americana

I used to have freckles, too.
Charming childhood imperfections still
glowing
On your fresh, clean face.
Tamed yet natural eyebrows
Framing bright, observant eyes.

I used to wear my hair up
Like yours, in a bouncy ponytail.
Silky hair, a mixture of corn crops and
sunshine,
Kept at bay with a black elastic;
Not harsh, but graceful.

And all those heritage brands you wear,
I can wear them too, just,
Your striped polo or cable knit sweater

Are crisp, put-together, ensembled.
And I, I'm just lumpy.

On summer days you're just as cheerful
As on dark, gloomy winter days.
Sweet pea season to vanilla season,
Khakis of high quality with boating shoes,
Or riding boots, or thick wooly socks.

Peaceful and harmonious, your family is
fiction.
But it isn't, you're all peach flesh and red
blood.
The chemistry you share enables you
To craft with dried pasta and
Eat hotdogs at baseball games without
getting fat.

American girl. The modern, urbanized
Rockwell.
Neat clothing, effortlessly worn;
Well-groomed, au naturel, perfumed.
Head-to-toe embodiment of a country's
values,
The poster-child of wealth.

NAHSHON COOK |

For People Confusing Black Men with Deer During Hunting Season: A Love Poem for George Zimmerman

1)   Last night, I sat in my room like a Mongolian lark looking out the window from behind the bars of its bamboo cage at a sparrow in the tree,--and feeling like a flower pot that never leaves the front porch, while I prayed to the muse, Erato, for a story that would make me human again. She arrived dressed a pair of big, carrot-orange butterfly wings outlined in white, polka-dotted black trim. After I'd grabbed something to write with, she recited this poem for me:

2)   I see you, She said, there, trying to look away from the convicting eyes of that nigger dangling from Lady Liberty's right wrist. The whip that jolted the buckboard forward and caused that nigger's neck to snap like a twig was the lions roar. In India they say: Sometimes the lion must roar to remind the horse of its fear. You won't be able to stop looking at that nigger until that nigger's body stops swaying in the breeze. Life is worth more than a price. That nigger is you.

3)   Stop running from your demons, She said. Demons are the shit from which angels bloom and heal the refugeed undead exiled in your heart--with love's true aloe, like a shaman. Goodbye.

STEPHEN PAUL MILLER |

Do you believe in Magic?

How about religion?

My favorite Taylor Mead poem is
The road to Philadelphia
Is paved with good intentions.

That's why New York HAS
NO road to Philadelphia.

Still, after all this time,
Just a bunch of roads.

To get there Ben Franklin just fucked it
And took a boat.

Ben was the Beatles before Charlie
Chaplin.

Taylor also left a hole
in culture's mattress
Whatever that means.

The Bible's Chewy Center

I'm actually writing poems that mean
something

(Unlike ones that do)

Pinch yourself

Don't tell

ANNE CARLY ABAD |

Jellyfish

Polyp

650 million years
planulae, cast adrift by strong currents,
attach to solid substrates in the sea,
the buds of a generation
> *Read the Good Book,*
> *kissed the first kiss,*
> *set myself to a dream*
> *of beauty, the art school*
> *I would later forget.*
> *I entwine the strings*
> *of my youth*
> *around my unripe pinkie.*

Bloom

The sea is hot and fertile
the ephyrae, detached
from their foundation,
go adrift in a slowly-
acidifying sea
> *I skim the shallows*
> *of how far I've come*
> *not far enough to succeed*
> *too far to be the person*
> *I want to be;*
> *work instead for the god*
> *of desks,*
> *tie more strings*
> *around too-few fingers.*

Migration

Though, not all drift.
The golden jellies
of Ongeim'l Tketau
recognize the light
love it, seek it

in order to survive
> *I wonder how*
> *my parents knew*
> *which one, when to stay*
> *when to leave,*
> *still together*
> *after all these years*
> *when what to live for*
> *is just another piece*
> *of debris floating*
> *in the sea.*

Predation

Jellyfish cannot poison
their own species
but they kill, at times devour
those not of their own
> *The boat is sinking faster*
> *and faster I throw out the old,*
> *the heavy, the useless.*
> *Is it too late to swim back*
> *to shore? Which string*
> *to pull and follow;*
> *how to stop grasping*
> *at every single thing*
> *that feels like salvation?*

Quallen

Polyp

650 Millionen Jahre
Planulae, auseinandergetrieben von
starken Strömungen,
halten fest an soliden Substraten im
Ozean,
Knospen einer Generation
> *Das Gute Buch gelesen,*
> *den ersten Kuss geküsst,*
> *habe einen Traum*

von Schönheit, die Kunsthochschule,
die ich später vergessen würde.
Ich umwickle mit den Fäden
meiner Jugend
meinen unreifen kleinen Finger.

Blume

Das Meer ist heiß und fruchtbar
die Ephyrae, getrennt
von ihrer Grundlage,
lassen sich treiben in einer langsam
versauernden See

Ich überfliege die Untiefen
wie weit bin ich gekommen
nicht weit genug, um es zu schaffen,
zu weit, um der Mensch zu sein,
der ich sein will;
arbeite stattdessen für den Gott
des Schreibtischs,
wickle noch mehr Fäden
um nicht genügend Finger.

Migration

Doch, nicht alle lassen sich treiben.
Die goldenen Quallen
von Ongeim'l Tketau
erkennen Licht
lieben es, streben danach
um zu überleben

Ich frage mich, woher
meine Eltern wussten,
wer, wann bleiben muss,
wann man gehen muss,
noch immer zusammen
nach all diesen Jahren
wenn das, wofür man lebt
nur wie ein weiteres Stück Schrott
im Ozean treibt.

Predation

Quallen vergiften niemals
ihre eigene Art
aber sie töten, verschlingen sogar
die, die nicht zu ihnen gehören

Das Schiff sinkt schneller
und schneller werfe ich Altes ab,
Schweres, Unnützes.
Ist es zu spät, zurückzuschwimmen
zur Küste? An welchem Faden
soll ich ziehen und ihm folgen;
wie ergreife ich nicht
jedes einzelne Ding
das sich wie Erlösung anfühlt?

Remains

The cracks are still here
woven into the grimy tiled floors
of the mall you no longer visit.
Though you should know
they're still here:

the stalls selling Nike imitations,
China-made clothes like clones,
tingi-tingi e-loading stations.
And he's still here—

The 99-Peso stylist
who almost cut off your ear
while spilling the latest gossip.

I'm here, listening to them argue
about new names and renovations

so nothing would be left of the old.

Überreste

Die Risse überziehen hier immer noch
den schmutzig gefliesten Fußboden
in dem Einkaufszentrum, das du nicht
mehr betrittst.
Aber du solltest wissen,
sie sind noch hier:

die Stände, die Nike-Fälschungen
verkaufen,
Kopien aus China wie Klone,
tingi-tingi Handylädchen.
Und er ist noch hier –

Der 99-Peso-Frisör,
der fast dein Ohr abgeschnitten hätte
als er den neuesten Tratsch erzählte.

Ich bin hier und höre zu, wie sie streiten
über neue Namen und Renovierungen
damit nichts vom Alten übrig bleibt.

Kenyatta Jean-Paul Garcia |

Would Go Well Here

From this perspective it is unknowable
and thought little of
but AM is just the erasing of
PM's ink being used to price
this soil, these farms, jungle, seven
wonders.

It's impossible to see the loop of zeros
beside the other numerals down here
but the gods who truly have a worldview
can throw down appraisals
and rollback costs
and cut deals with each other
and split nations and states at will
for gerrymandered purposes.

Why else would India be thrust into Asia?
And South America have a little taken off
its tip?

And it is called melting here but above, it
is said,
"a little more water would go well here –
for a new tourist trap."

Würde Sich Hier Gut Machen

Aus dieser Perspektive kann man es nicht
sehen
und es wird kaum bedacht
aber der Morgen löscht einfach die
Tinte des Abends, der sonst die Preise
angibt
für diesen Boden, diese Farmen,
Dschungel, sieben Wunder.

Unmöglich erkennt man die Schlinge der
Nullen
neben den anderen Zahlzeichen hier
unten
aber die Götter, die die Welt ganz sehen,
können Einschätzungen runterschleudern
und die Kosten senken
und Vereinbarungen treffen
und Nationen und Länder willkürlich
spalten
mit korrupten Zielen.

Warum sonst sollte Indien in Asien
hineingerammt werden?
Und Südamerika etwas von seiner Spitze
abgeben?

Und hier nennt man es Schmelzen, aber
oben sagt man,
„etwas mehr Wasser würde sich hier gut
machen –
als neue Touristenfalle.“

ARNDT BRITSCHGI |

Trichet-Tricheur

In an interview with the French Europe
1radio station, former ECB President
Jean-Claude Trichet gives his view of the
economic crisis in Europe, particularly its
southern, Mediterranean countries. The
interview is transmitted early on Sunday
morning, you listen to Trichet's analysis
with a certain interest and measure of
unhurried concentration. His core
argument can be summed up in two or
three basic sentences.

The roots of the present crisis are in
highly exaggerated public spending, with
ensuing high debt levels and national
budget deficits. When the rest of the
world won't continue to finance the
deficits of the indebted countries, these
have to regain their stability or balance
progressively, by systematically cutting
their expenses. They have to implement
reforms and maintain austerity efforts to
regain the confidence of the investors,
without the actual rates of margin that less
indebted countries can allow themselves.
The interviewer asks Trichet if these
politics haven't led to an impoverishment
of the broader populations in the South,
through no real fault of their own, and
Trichet admits this in part: it's the leaders,
not the citizens at large who are to blame
for the erroneous decisions. But we have
to remember that, as these countries have
behaved badly in the past, their citizens
too have enjoyed the advantages of the
short-term benefits produced; so it's only
natural that they pay back what at an
earlier stage they received.

Trichet takes the example of Germany, who in the 1990's, due to its weak economy earned itself a name as "the sick man of Europe." Germany wasn't sick but potentially sound, through its reforms and severe saving measures laying the foundations of its future growth. It took Germany 10 years of struggling to recover economically, but now its unemployment is marginal and its financial basis solid. Here the interviewer points out that much of the labor-market recovery has come in terms of "minijobs" and near-minimum-wage employments which have aggravated the conditions of the working force, but Trichet dismisses this: mass unemployment, in creating inequality, lack of social cohesion and high rates of criminality, is the worst possible perspective, any measure that avoids it must be considered a success. And this is basically what Germany through its austerity has achieved; now the other, southern countries are in line.

Trichet's narrative is seducingly simple and intelligible, you find yourself intuitively disposed or even eager to accept it. The high-debt countries spend too much, their welfare bills surpass the Germans' to considerable degrees (in case of France specifically: by 10%). Their economies show very little flexibility (labor agreements and protection are too generous); their "competitivity" is low (production costs and wages are too high). For years and years Germany battled to reduce these same defects, saving while other countries overspent, it's comfortable to think that now the Germans prosper while the others pay the prize for their transgressions. Your moral attitudes are flattered by this reassuring truth. But as the morning passes on and

you reluctantly wake up the thinking self inside of you starts to react.

For if it's true that Germany by now has durably recovered – not just transferred its previous debt into a massive, concealed poverty among its broader ranks, but reached a state of healthy economic growth – if this is true, then by what means did it achieve it? By its exports, it would seem. And the ones who did a grand part of the buying, who were they? The southern European countries obviously. Wasn't it Germany encouraging its neighbors from the South to spend more money, take more loans (from German banks, preferably, not always necessarily at favorable overall conditions), to invest freely in all kinds of enterprises, sane or not, which would increase the slow demand for German products, new equipment and supplies, providing orders for its industry and growing, lucrative markets. It was like this – by purposely provoking just the kind of reckless, immeasurably puffed up, slack economic behavior which they now accuse the southern countries of – more than anything, like this Germany overcame the crisis it had gladly caused itself while financing its unification. Instead of paying back the favor, what it asks its neighbors now are sacrifices which will serve to help sustain its proper exports, first of all, and something more. It inexorably demands to get the loans paid back in full, meaning the southern countries end up paying doubly for its wealth, once by buying and investing in its goods, opening markets, once the interest exacted to afford such deals at all. Without vast loans the southern countries never could have entered in; and so the narrative Trichet sells proves a huge and ugly myth.

This is revolting in itself, and even more so when you think that, since you realize these facts, Trichet must realize them too. And since he does, what you conclude is that he's consciously dishonest. So then the next thing you'll be asking is, whose interests does he run (except, in secondary sense, his own)? What are his motives, what is driving him to act the way he does? You take a look at the statistics and you learn that, once again, whereas the wages and conditions of the masses have gone down, whereas the crisis makes its victims by the millions companies of every order boost their profits on and on, from year to year – and money doesn't disappear, we know, but merely changes hands. The benefits that are produced have to exist, they must be somewhere. Trichet is cheating, he's a liar, but no major driving force: he seems to carry out a scheme of larger scope that lies beneath, on account of some vague forces that we're not able to name, in command of what is basically an ideological-economic war.

Trichet-Tricheur

In einem Interview mit dem französischen Radiosender Europe 1 legt ex-EZB-Präsident Jean-Claude Trichet seine Meinung zur europäischen Wirtschaftskrise, besonders bezüglich der südeuropäischen Mittelmeerländer, dar. Das Interview wird früh am Sonntagmorgen ausgestrahlt, man hört Trichets Analyse mit einem gewissen Interesse und entspannter Konzentration zu. Der Kern seiner Argumentation kann in zwei, drei grundlegenden Thesen zusammengefasst werden.

Grund für die derzeitige Krise sind die übermäßigen öffentlichen Ausgaben mit sich daraus ergebender hoher Verschuldung und staatliche Haushaltsdefizite. Wenn die übrigen Länder nicht mehr bereit sind, die Defizite der verschuldeten Staaten auszugleichen, müssen diese schrittweise ihre Stabilität oder ihr Gleichgewicht wiederfinden, indem sie systematisch ihre Ausgaben verringern. Sie müssen Reformen durchsetzen und Sparmaßnahmen aufrechterhalten, um das Vertrauen ihrer Investoren zurückzugewinnen, ohne das übliche Maß an Spielraum, das sich weniger verschuldete Länder erlauben können. Der Moderator fragt Trichet, ob diese Politik nicht zu einer Verarmung breiter Bevölkerungsschichten Südeuropas ohne deren eigenes Verschulden geführt habe, und Trichet gesteht dies teilweise zu. Es sind zwar die Regierungen, nicht die Bürger, die für die falschen Entscheidungen verantwortlich sind, aber wir dürfen nicht vergessen, dass, indem sich diese Länder in der Vergangenheit schlecht benommen haben, auch ihre Bevölkerungen aus dem kurzfristig erzielten Gewinn einen Nutzen gezogen haben; es ist gewissermaßen natürlich, dass sie jetzt begleichen, was sie vorher erhalten haben.

Trichet nimmt Deutschland als Beispiel. In den 90er Jahren wurde Deutschland aufgrund seiner schwachen Wirtschaft als "der kranke Mann Europas" bezeichnet. Aber Deutschland war nicht krank, sondern, indem es sich durch Reformen und eine strenge Sparpolitik eine Grundlage für sein zukünftiges Wachstum legte, potentiell gesund. Deutschland musste 10 Jahre lang kämpfen, um sich wirtschaftlich zu erholen; heute ist die Arbeitslosigkeit niedrig und die finanzielle Grundlage stabil. Der Moderator gibt hier zu bedenken, dass ein Großteil der Arbeitsmarkterholung auf "Minijobs" und Quasi-Mindestlohnbeschäftigungen zurückzuführen sei, aber Trichet weist diesen Einwand zurück. Massenarbeitslosigkeit fördere Ungleichheit, mangelnden sozialen Zusammenhalt und Kriminalität und sei somit die schlechteste aller möglichen Perspektiven; jegliche Maßnahme, die das verhindere, müsse als Erfolg betrachtet werden. Und das sei es grundsätzlich, was Deutschland durch seine Sparsamkeit zustande gebracht habe; jetzt seien die Länder Südeuropas an der Reihe.

Trichets Darlegung ist verführerisch einfach und einleuchtend, man ist intuitiv geneigt, sogar begierig, ihr zuzustimmen. Die hochverschuldeten Länder verschwenden zu viel, ihre Sozialausgaben übertreffen diejenigen Deutschlands beträchtlich (allein in Frankreich um 10%). Ihre Wirtschaftssysteme zeigen wenig Flexibilität (Tarifverträge und Arbeitsschutz sind zu großzügig); ihre Konkurrenzfähigkeit ist niedrig (Produktionskosten und Löhne sind zu hoch). Ein Jahrzehnt lang musste Deutschland kämpfen, um genau diese Schwächen zu minimieren. Es hat gespart, während andere Länder Geld ausgaben. Es ist angenehm zu sehen, wie die Deutschen jetzt profitieren, während die anderen den Preis für ihre Fehler zahlen. Die eigenen Moralvorstellungen werden durch diese beruhigende Wahrheit bestätigt. Aber im Laufe des Morgens, wenn man langsam wacher wird, fängt das denkende Ich in einem an, zu reagieren.

Denn wenn es stimmt, dass sich Deutschland mittlerweile dauerhaft erholt hat – und nicht nur seine früheren Schulden in eine massive, versteckte Armut unter den breiten Schichten umstrukturiert hat, sondern zu einem wahren Zustand von finanziellem Wachstum gelangt ist – wenn das stimmt, auf welchem Wege hat es das dann erreicht? Durch Exporte, wie es scheint. Und diejenigen, die die Rolle des Importeurs übernahmen, wer waren die? Zum großen Teil die südeuropäischen Länder. War es nicht Deutschland, das seine Nachbarn im Süden ermunterte, mehr Geld auszugeben, dafür mehr Kredite aufzunehmen (vorzugsweise von deutschen Banken, nicht immer unbedingt unter günstigen Gesamtbedingungen), reichlich in Projekte aller Art zu investieren, vernünftig oder nicht, die die Nachfrage nach deutschen Produkten, neuen Einrichtungen und Materialien steigern würden, die mehr Aufträge für die Industrie und wachsende, lukrative Märkte zur Folge hätten? Auf diese Weise – durch absichtliche Unterstützung von genau derartig unbekümmertem, maßlos aufgepumptem finanziellem Verhalten, das es den südeuropäischen Ländern jetzt vorwirft – vor allem auf diese Weise hat Deutschland seine Krise, die es selbst sorglos durch die Wiedervereinigung herbeigeführt hatte, überwunden. Statt jetzt den Gefallen zurückzugeben, verlangt es jetzt erst einmal größere Opfer von seinen Nachbarn, um die eigenen Exporte aufrechtzuerhalten, und, zweitens, unerbittlich alle ausstehenden Kredite ungekürzt zurück, wodurch die südeuropäischen Staaten am Ende zweifach für den deutschen Wohlstand zahlen, einmal, weil sie in seine Güter investieren und neue Märkte eröffnen, einmal, weil sie die Zinsen, die solche Geschäfte überhaupt erst ermöglichen, entrichten. Ohne die hohen Kredite hätten die südeuropäischen Länder gar nicht mitmachen können – Trichets Bericht erweist sich als nichts als eine große, üble Lüge.

Das ist an sich schon empörend, aber umso mehr, wenn man bedenkt, dass, wenn man diesen Umstand selbst versteht, Trichet ihn dann ebenso gut kennt. Und weil er das tut, muss man folgern, dass er bewusst unaufrichtig ist. Was man sich dann als Nächstes fragt, ist, wessen Interessen er dabei vertritt (außer, im sekundären Sinne, seine eigenen). Was hat er für Gründe, was motiviert ihn, so zu handeln wie er handelt? Man schaut sich die Statistik an und erfährt, dass, während die Löhne und Lebensbedingungen der breiten Masse einmal mehr gesunken sind, und die Krise ihre Opfer in Millionen zählt, Unternehmen aller Art jahrein, jahraus hohe Gewinne erwirtschaften – und, wie wir wissen, Geld verschwindet nicht, es wechselt einfach nur den Besitzer. Die Profite sind real, sie müssen immer noch irgendwo sein. Trichet betrügt uns, er ist ein Lügner, aber längst nicht der Hauptakteur: Er scheint einen umfangreichen untergründigen Plan umzusetzen, im Namen unbekannter Machthaber, die wir nicht ganz ausmachen können, und führt im Grunde einen ideologisch-ökonomischen Krieg.

Contributors | Beitragende

Angela S. Patane is a writer, teacher, and musician residing in Southwest Florida. | **Angela S. Patane**, die derzeit im Südwesten Floridas lebt, ist eine Schriftstellerin, Lehrerin und Musikerin.

Anthony Keating is a poet from Kentish Town, North London, who is currently living in West Lancashire following 15 years in Dublin. | **Anthony Keating** ist ein Poet aus Kentish Town im Norden Londons, der momentan in West Lancashire lebt, nachdem er 15 Jahre in Dublin verbracht hat.

Bart Bultman was born in 1986 in Austin, Texas. He graduated from Hope College and currently lives in West Michigan. | **Bart Bultman** wurde 1986 in Austin (Texas/USA) geboren. Er hat einen Abschluss vom Hope College und lebt derzeit in West Michigan.

Chris Siteman grew up in Boston in a predominantly Irish-Catholic family. He has traveled widely in the US and Europe and worked extensively in the trades. Currently he teaches in Suffolk University's English department. | **Chris Siteman** wurde in Boston geboren, wo er in einer zum überwiegenden Teil irisch-katholischen Familie aufgewachsen ist. Derzeit unterrichtet er am Lehrstuhl für Englisch an der Suffolk University.

Colleen M. Farrelly is a graduate student at University of Miami and freelance writer. | **Colleen M. Farrelly** ist Masterstudentin an der Universität in Miami und freischaffende Schriftstellerin.

Darian Lane was born in Philadelphia, Pennsylvania and raised in Bethesda, Maryland. He graduated from Arizona State University and moved to Los Angeles to produce and help direct music videos and commercials. | **Darian Lane** ist in Philadelphia (Pennsylvania) geboren und in Bethesda (Maryland) in den USA aufgewachsen. Nach seinem Abschluss an der Arizona State University ist er nach Los Angeles gezogen wo er als Regieassistent Musikvideos und Werbung produziert.

Jeanine Deibel is an MFA Candidate in Poetry at NMSU where she teaches Creative Writing and works as a Managing Editor for Puerto del Sol. | **Jeanine Deibel** ist Masterstudentin mit Schwerpunkt Lyrik an der NMSU, an der sie ebenfalls kreatives Schreiben unterrichtet und die Puerto del Sol herausgibt.

Joe Dresner was born in Sunderland in 1987 and now lives and works in London. | Joe Dresner wurde 1987 in Sunderland in Großbritannien geboren und lebt heute in London.

Mark Farrell is from Nova Scotia, Canada and has been living in the Czech Republic for over fifteen years. He teaches at Charles University in Prague. Mark's work has appeared in many journals throughout the world. | **Mark Farrell** kommt aus Nova Scotia, Kanada, lebt allerdings bereits seit fünfzehn Jahren in Tschechien, wo er an der Charles University in Prag unterrichtet. Marks literarische Arbeiten sind in verschiedensten Magazinen weltweit erschienen.

Martha Clarkson is a photographer, writer, and designer in Seattle, Washington, USA. | **Martha Clarkson**

ist eine Schriftstellerin, Fotografin und Designerin aus Seattle, Washington, USA.

Nicholas Komodore is a Greek poet, filmmaker, photographer, and composer from Athens, currently living and working in Oakland. He started Mayakov+sky, a collaborative platform on poetics and architecture. His work has been featured internationally in festivals, exhibitions, galleries, and literary magazines. | **Nicholas Komodore** ist ein griechischer Poet, Filmemacher, Fotograf und Komponist aus Athen. Momentan lebt und arbeitet er in Oakland. Er hat das Projekt Mayakov+sky ins Leben gerufen, eine kollaborative Plattform über Lyrik und Architektur. Seine Arbeiten sind auf Festivals, Ausstellungen, Gallerien und in Literaturzeitschriften erschienen.

Nicolas Poynter is a chemist and teaches AP physics in high school. He is currently working on his MFA in creative writing. | **Nicolas Poynter** ist Chemiker und unterrichtet Physik an einer high school. Im Moment arbeitet er an seinem MFA in kreativem Schreiben.

Richard O'Connell lives in Hillsboro Beach, Florida. Collections of his poetry include RetroWorlds, Simulations, Voyages and The Bright Tower. His work has appeared in numerous magazines. | **Richard O'Connell** lebt in Hillsboro Beach, Florida. Auszüge seiner Texte sind in den Büchern Retro Worlds, Simulations, Voyages und The Bright Tower erschienen. Seine Texte sind in zahlreichen Magazinen veröffentlicht.

Rita D. Costello (originally from New York) has lived all over America and China. She is the Director of Freshman and Sophomore English at McNeese State University in Louisiana and co-editor of the anthology Bend Don't Shatter. Her work has appeared in various journals. | **Rita D. Costello**, geboren in New York, hat schon in den verschiedensten Staaten der USA sowie in China gelebt. Sie ist die Leiterin des Freshman and Sophomore Centers für Englisch an der McNeese State University of Louisiana und Mitherausgeberin der Anthologie Bend Don't Shatter. Ihre Texte sind in verschiedenen Journalen veröffentlicht.

Ryan Negrini is a creative writing consultant at Valencia College in Orlando, Florida. | **Ryan Negrini** ist Student im Creative Writing Programm des Valencia Colleges in Orlando, Florida.

Saïdeh Pakravan is an Iranian-American (but French-educated) author of fiction, poetry, and essays. Her work has appeared in numerous literary magazines as well as anthologies and she is a frequent speaker on Iran. | **Saïdeh Pakravan** ist eine Amerikanisch-Iranisch stämmige (allerdings in Frankreich ausgebildete) Schriftstellerin. Ihre Texte sind in zahlreichen Literaturmagazinen und Anthologien veröffentlicht worden und sie trägt regelmäßig über den Iran vor.

Sam Smith is the editor of The Journal (once 'of Contemporary Anglo-Scandinavian Poetry') and publisher of Original Plus books. At the moment living in Maryport, Cumbria, he has several poetry collections and novels to his name. | **Sam Smith** ist der Herausgeber des Magazins "The Journal" (früher "Zeitgenössische Anglo-Skandinavische Poesie") und Verleger der Original Plus books. Sam hat mehrere Gedichtbände und Romane veröffentlicht und lebt derzeit in Maryport, Cumbria in Großbritannien.

Makings of a Maniac are a poetry & music act from Doncaster, operating out of Manchester, UK. They comprise of **Sam Wainwright** & **Dan Welsh**. Sam and Dan met at a knackered old school in Donny through Dan's cousin and have become embittered by modern life at approximately the same rate. So at a loss of what to do they did the only thing they had left - performance poetry laced with funky hip-hop beats. | **Makings of Maniac** sind ein Poetry- & Musik-Duo aus Doncaster, das in Manchester aktiv ist. **Sam Wainwright** und **Dan Welsh** haben sich in einer verwahrlosten, alten Schule in "Donny" (Doncaster, England) durch Dans Cousin kennen gelernt. Im Rahmen ihrer Freundschaft mussten sie zu gleichen Teilen mit der immer moderner werdenden Welt um sie herum klar kommen. Da sie kaum einen Plan hatten, wie sie darauf reagieren sollten, machten sie das Einzige, was ihnen plausibel erschien und begannen performance poetry mit funky-gen Hip Hop Beats zu mixen und produzieren.

Makings of a Maniac are a poetry & music act from Doncaster, operating out of Manchester, UK. They comprise **Sam Wainwright** & **Dan Welsh** and perform poetry laced with funky hip-hop beats. | **Makings of Maniac** sind ein Poetry- & Musik-Duo aus Doncaster, das in Manchester aktiv ist: **Sam Wainwright** und **Dan Welsh** betreiben performance poetry und mixen diese mit funky-gen Hip Hop Beats.

Sophia Cosby is a German-American studying in Scotland, but is currently on a year abroad in Vienna. | **Sophia Cosby** ist Amerikanerin deutscher Herkunft, studiert in Schottland und macht derzeit ein Auslandsjahr in Wien.

Nahshon Cook is an American poet. His second book, "The Killing Fields and Other Poems" will be published in 2015 by Sabda Press. | **Nahshon Cook** ist ein amerikanischer Poet, sein nächster Gedichtband "The Killing Fields and Other Poems" wird 2015 bei Sabda Press erscheinen.

Stephen Paul Miller is the author of several books including The Seventies Now: Culture as Surveillance (Duke University Press) and poetry books including There's Only One God and You're Not It (Marsh Hawk Press). | **Stephen Paul Miller** ist Autor mehrerer Bücher, unter anderen The Seventies Now: Culture as Surveillance (Duke University Press) oder des Gedichtbands There's Only One God and You're Not It (Marsh Hawk Press).

Anne Carly Abad writes poetry and stories when she's not training Muay Thai. | **Anne Carly Abad** schreibt Gedichte und Geschichten wenn sie nicht gerade Muay Thai trainiert.

Jeff Harris is founder of the Lefty Jones Band and has written four books. "Fay & Eddy", "The Smiley-Man Chronicles", "Church of the Red Arrow" (under the pen-name of Michael Houlihan), and the "Forgotten Papers" from which "The minutia of budget" is taken. | **Jeff Harris** ist Gründer der Lefty Jones Band und hat vier Bücher geschrieben: "Fay & Eddy", "The Smiley-Man Chronicles", "Church of the Red Arrow" (unter dem Pseudonym Michael Houlihan), und die "Forgotten Papers" aus denen der im the

Transnational erschienene Auszug "The minutia of budget" stammt.

Kenyatta Jean-Paul Garcia is the author of Yawning on the Sands, This Sentimental Education and Enter the After-Garde along with other collections of poetry. He was raised in Brooklyn, NY and has a degree in Linguistics. After many years as a cook, he has returned to poetry. His work has appeared in BlazeVOX, Caliban Online, Ink, Sweat and Tears, ditch, Outlaw Poetry Network and Ron Silliman's Blog. He also writes for and edits kjpgarcia.wordpress.com and altpoetics.wordpress.com. |

Kenyatta Jean-Paul Garcia ist der Autor der Lyrikbände Yawning on the Sands, This Sentimental Education und Enter the After-Garde. Er ist in Brooklyn in New York aufgewachsen und hat einen Abschluss in Linguistik. Nachdem er jahrelang als Koch gearbeitet hat, hat er wieder angefangen sich der Poesie zu widmen. Seine Texte sind erschienen in BlazeVOX, Caliban Online, Ink, Sweat and Tears, ditch, Outlaw Poetry Network und Ron Silliman's Blog. Über dies hinaus schreibt er für kjpgarcia.wordpress.com und ist Herausgeber der altpoetics.wordpress.com.

Arndt Britschgi was born and raised in Finland. He spent the best part of his life in Madrid (Spain) and completed his Ph.D. in Philosophy from the University of Zürich (Switzerland) in 2006. His books on Newcomb's Paradox/Free Will is available in English from Philosophia Verlag in Germany. | **Arndt Britschgi** ist in Finnland geboren und aufgewachsen. Die beste Zeit seines Lebens hat er jedoch in Madrid (Spanien) verbracht. 2006 schloss er seine Promotion in Philosophie

an der Züricher Universität ab. Sein Buch über Newcomb's Problem (Entscheidungstheorie) ist im Philosophia Verlag in Deutschland erschienen.

Transnational – The Team

Seong-Ho Kwak has spent the last decade acquainting himself with the vagaries of German grammar. This involved taking a German degree, thanks to which he was able to spend a wild and wonderful year abroad in Berlin. For a couple of years following his graduation, he lost himself in the corporate wilderness. Now, he works at a lovely London-based translation company and hasn't looked back since. | **Seong-Ho Kwak** hat das letzte Jahrzehnt damit verbracht, sich mit den Launen der deutschen Grammatik vertraut zu machen. Das brachte die Erlangung eines Deutsch-Abschlusses mit sich, aufgrund dessen er ein wildes und wunderbares Jahr in Berlin verbrachte. Nach seinem Abschluss verlor er sich für ein Paar Jahre im Dschungel der Geschäftswelt. Heute arbeitet er für eine Übersetzungsagentur mit Sitz in London und hat seitdem nicht mehr zurückgeschaut.

Ariane Enkelmann liest, schreibt und denkt bilingual. In ihrem Deutsch- und Englischstudium an der Leibniz Universität Hannover lernte sie, dass sogar e.e. cummings übersetzt werden kann. Seitdem ist sie auf der Suche nach poetischen und linguistischen Herausforderungen. Sie war in Deutschland, Alabama, China und Kanada zu Hause. Jetzt lebt und studiert sie in Berlin. | **Ariane Enkelmann** reads, writes and thinks bilingual. While she studied German and English at Leibniz University Hanover she discovered that even e.e. cummings can be translated. Ever since, she's been looking for poetic and linguistic challenges. She has called Germany, Alabama, China, and Canada her home. Now she lives and studies in Berlin.

Dennis Staats wurde 1983 in Kärnten geboren. Er studierte Vergleichende Literaturwissenschaft an der Universität Wien. Während seines Studiums arbeitete er als freier Journalist und versuchte sich an seinem ersten Roman. Er schrieb seine Abschlussarbeit über die Rezeption der Romane Jack Kerouacs im deutschen Sprachraum. Nach seinem Studium arbeitete er als PR-Manager sowie als Projektleiter in einer internationalen Marketingagentur in Wien und Zürich. Zu dieser Zeit entstanden mehrere Kurzgeschichten und Gedichte. Dennis Staats lebt und arbeitet in Kärnten. | **Dennis Staats** was born in Carinthia, Austria in 1983. He studied comparative literature at the University of Vienna. While he was at university he worked as a journalist for several newspapers and wrote his first novel. He wrote his master thesis on the reception of Jack Kerouac's novels in the German speaking world. After graduation he worked as a PR manager and as a project manager at an international marketing agency in Vienna and Zurich. During this time he wrote several short stories and poems. Dennis Staats lives and works in Carinthia.

A special THANK YOU goes to **Barbara Marcantonio** who designed the logo for the Transnational!

Sarah Katharina Kayß hat Geschichtswissenschaften, Vergleichenden Religionswissenschaften und britische Kolonialgeschichte in Deutschland und Großbritannien studiert. Seit Herbst 2012 ist sie Promotionsstudentin am War Studies Department am King's College in London. Ihre Fotografien, Gedichte und Essays sind veröffentlicht in Deutschland, der Schweiz, Österreich, Großbritannien, Italien, Neuseeland, den USA und Kanada. Sie ist Preisträgerin der Manuskriptförderung des Literaturwerk Rheinland-Pfalz-Saar und dem Verband Deutscher Schriftsteller (2013). 2014 erscheint ihr Gedicht- und Prosaband „Ich mag die Welt so wie sie ist" bei Allitera in München. Sarah ist Herausgeberin des Transnational (ehemals: PostPoetry) - und lebt seit Sommer 2010 in London. | **Sarah Katharina Kayß** studied Comparative Religion and Modern History in Germany and Britain. In autumn 2012, she became a PhD candidate at the War Studies Department of King's College London. Her artwork, essays and poetry have appeared in Germany, Switzerland, Austria, the United Kingdom, Italy, Canada, New Zealand and the United States. Sarah is a winner of the manuscript-award of the German Writers Association (2013). Her poetry and essay collection "Ich mag die Welt so wie sie ist" (I like the world the way it is) will be published in 2014. She edits The Transnational (former: PostPoetry) and lives in London.

We'd like to thank all the authors who have made this issue possible!

Unser herzlicher Dank geht an alle Autoren, die diese Ausgabe möglich gemacht haben!

CPSIA information can be obtained
at www.ICGtesting.com
Printed in the USA
BVHW051925120320
574846BV00004B/327